THE SURVIVALIST

#1

TOTAL WAR

The Survivalist Series
By Jerry Ahern

THE SURVIVALIST

#1

TOTAL WAR

JERRY AHERN

SPEAKING VOLUMES, LLC

NAPLES, FL

2011

THE SURVIVALIST

#1: TOTAL WAR

ISBN 978-1-61232-239-1

For Sharon, Jason, and Samantha
—who've survived a whole hell of a lot with me
—love always.

Foreword

"Everyone look away from the windows and put your heads down! Protect your faces, your eyes!"

Rourke's cries were too late—the plane was already caught in the path of the nuclear warhead. From the windows, Rourke could see what was left of the destroyed city of St. Louis—but the moans and screams of the passengers kept his thoughts away from the devastation outside.

He climbed over wounded people to reach the pilot's cabin. Both the captain and co-pilot were still strapped in their seats, writhing and holding their faces.

"My God, both these men are blinded like—"

Rourke leaned down beside the pilot and said, "I'm one of the passengers. If you can stay conscious, maybe you can tell me what to do to keep this thing airborne."

"That's impossible. The controls on these babies are just too much unless you know them—I can't talk you through it."

"Well, I don't figure we've got more than a couple of hours flying time before we hit empty. And auto pilot isn't going to do much good next time we hit a shock wave from a missile going off under us!"

Rourke glanced at the thick, vinyl-bound manuals in the cockpit. "I think I can fly her—but what happens when it's time to land?" he thought to himself, looking at the ruins below . . .

Chapter One

"Now!" Rourke shouted, pushing himself up from a low crouch and waving his left arm. He burst into a long-strided, loping run down the steep gravel embankment, past the scattered granite outcroppings, and toward the packed dirt highway below. The dozen men close behind him wore the khaki fatigues of the Pakistani Counter-Terrorist Strike Force. Fierce threats of death and violence issued from them. Small H-K MP5SD3 integral silencer, collapsible stock 9-mm submachine guns in their white-knuckled fists, they stormed the two dozen turban-clad opium smugglers on the highway, clinging to the four stake trucks.

As Rourke's strike force reached the midway point to the highway, the smugglers began returning fire. Oil-smeared tarps were whisked from then heavy machine guns mounted on tripods in the back of each of the opium-packed truck beds. Small-arms fire bristled from the opened windows and doors.

Rourke fired the Heckler & Koch P2A1 flare pistol clenched in his right hand. Its 26.5-mm projectile soared high into the gray winter sky, then exploded.

From his vantage point along the embankment, Rourke could see the heavily armored Pakistani military half-track moving into position and blocking the road about half a mile further down the mountain. Stuffing the emptied flare pistol into the outside pocket of the borrowed leather sheepskin coat he wore, Rourke swung his own H-K SMG into a firing position, then ran down the last hundred yards of the embankment, leading his men and firing.

Already, he could see the lead vehicle of the four-truck caravan swerving into a U-turn under the withering machine gun fire from the half-track. Two of its wheels spun precariously near the ditch on the near side of the road, then the truck lumbered back onto the road, coming toward him. Emptying the H-K's thirty-round magazine Rourke crossed the road in a dead run, then hit the gravel on the drop-off side of the road, and threw down the H-K. His right hand, then his left, reached for one, then another of the brace of stainless steel Detonics .45 autos from under his coat.

Thumbing back the hammer on the scaled-down .45 in his right hand, he closed his fist tightly over the rubber Pachmayr grips. He triggered one round toward the cab of the truck. The pistol in his left hand spit fire at the same instant. Both shots connected. The driver's body bounced away from the wheel.

Rourke rolled back from the lip of the highway, sliding down along the edge of the steep slope. The truck was out of control and careening toward him. As it rocketed over the edge of the road, Rourke fired his pistols into the fuel tank, and the truck exploded. The blistering flames of the fireball scorched his face.

Glancing up toward the highway, clambering along the slope, Rourke spotted one of the three remaining trucks going into a skid, half climbing the embankment and flipping onto its side. The fortune in opium that was its cargo spilled out along the highway. The guard from the truck's passenger seat tried to climb out the window, but stopped halfway and brought up a stubby muzzled submachine gun to spray the roadside.

Rourke saw two of his newest strike force men go down. Dropping and skidding on both knees toward the truck, Rourke fired both Detonics .45's. The sub-gunner turned toward him, and Rourke fired twice again. The sub-gunner's upper torso snapped back, the automatic weapon in his hands flew skyward, his body bent at a tortuous angle.

Rourke got to his feet and ran down the road toward the two stopped trucks. More than a dozen smugglers were exchanging automatic-weapons fire with the half-track. "Grenades!" Rourke shouted over his shoulder to the men running close behind him. There was a belching roar from one of the H-K 69's. Its 40-mm high-explosive projective whistled overhead. Rourke dropped to the road, tucking his head down as the grenade exploded just yards in front of him. He glanced up as the truck exploded. Bodies and severed arms and legs soared into the air. The sky rained opium and bloody flesh. One of the H-K 69's whooshed again. The second truck exploded.

Pushing himself up onto his elbows, then getting to his feet, Rourke shouted to his men, "Finish 'em!" His team closed in on the surviving drug runners. He fired both Detonics pistols until they went empty, then stuffed them into the waistband of his trousers and reached to his hip for the Metalifed six-inch Colt

Python .357 holstered there, firing it point blank into the chest of the closest of the drug smugglers, then emptied it into two more of the men coming at him.

Using his empty Colt like a truncheon, he smashed down hard on the head of the nearest of the smugglers, then wheeled around. A turban-clad man with a long-bladed knife charged toward him. Rourke sidestepped. He dropped the Python back into its holster—no time to reload. As the Pakistani smuggler charged toward him again, Rourke edged back and grabbed his A.G. Russell Sting IA boot knife.

The smuggler slowed, then dove forward. Rourke sidestepped the knife and whipped down with his small, double-edged blade against the right side of the man's neck, slicing open an artery. Wheeling again, Rourke drew his right arm up, deflecting a blow from another nearby smuggler. He lost his blade and now, tucked into a crouch, his left fist smashed up, into the Pakistani's stomach, while his right hand knifed forward, palm upward, fingers extended. The blow connected with his attacker's throat and crushed the windpipe. Then, wheeling around, in the classic T-stance, Rourke stopped.

To his left, one of his men was knocking the last drug dealer down to the road with the butt of his sub gun.

Drawing up his shoulders, Rourke breathed deeply. Turning and snatching one of the spare six-round magazines from a double pouch at his trouser belt, Rourke dropped the empty magazine from one of the Detonics .45s into his hand, rammed the fresh magazine home and worked the slide stop, stripping the top round and loading the chamber. Carefully, he lowered the little stainless gun's bobbed hammer and then slipped it into the speed break holster under his left arm.

As Rourke started reloading the second pistol, he glanced up at the sound of the familiar voice.

"Your men—and you, yourself, John Thomas, were superb!"

A smile lighting the brown eyes in his lean, clean shaven face, Rourke said, "From you, Captain, that's the finest of compliments. But we lost two. They bunched together—I warned them not to."

The other man nodded.

3

Rourke added, "But maybe the others'll learn by it. You and I both know that the stuff that's hardest to remember is the stuff that'll usually keep you alive or get you killed."

"You're right, John Thomas. But I think these men you trained will do well in this opium war we fight." The Pakistani captain, shorter than Rourke and with a bushy black moustache, lit a cigarette for himself, then offered one to Rourke.

"No, thanks, Muhammed," Rourke muttered, then reached into his shirt pocket and plucked a tiny cigar and put it between his teeth. "I'll take a light though," he said, leaning toward the Pakistani's cupped hands, sucking in the flame of the match, then leaning back and exhaling the gray smoke slowly. He watched it catch on the wind and blow down along the road to vanish where two of the trucks still smoldered.

Rourke ran the fingers of his left hand through his dark brown hair, pushing it back from his high forehead. "You still planning a mop-up operation here?"

Hunching his shoulders against the raw wind, the Pakistani nodded. "I think then that it is good-bye for you to your men."

"Yeah, I guess you're right," Rourke said, glancing over his shoulder as he finished loading six fresh rounds into the cylinder of the Python, then putting it back into its holster on his right hip. "Hang on a minute," Rourke told the Pakistani, then turned and walked back up the road toward the ten men remaining from his force.

The young military policemen came to attention as Rourke approached, but he gestured for them to remain at ease. "You guys did good," he said. "That's why you're still alive. Muli and Achmed—they didn't remember what I taught you guys, and that's why they're dead. They were good men, no worse, no better than any of you here. I want you to understand that. Surviving—whether it's a fight like this or just gettin' home at night in traffic means keeping your head, remembering what you're supposed to do, learning to react the way you know you should—then just doing it. I won't be seeing you guys again. I told you, I've gotta get back to the states. Maybe someday we'll all get together again. And if you guys remember that the first rule—in this or anything in life—is to keep your head, you'll all be alive so that we can get together."

Rourke shook hands with each of the men, a longer handshake for the corporal, Ahmed. At first, Rourke had confused the man with Achmed because of the similarities of their names. "Good luck, pal," Rourke whispered, clasping his shoulder and returning the warm smile in his eyes. "Here," he added impulsively, handing the man the Heckler & Koch flare pistol from his pocket. "You're the team leader now. You'll be needing this."

Rourke turned and walked back toward Muhammed. The helicopter coming for them was already looming large on the horizon, the distant whirring of its rotor blades like the drone of an insect.

They waited together, Rourke and Muhammed, without speaking. The helicopter hovered over the mountain road a moment, then angled down and landed—uncomfortably close, Rourke thought, to the embankment.

He ran around to the starboard side of the machine and slid in beside the pilot. Muhammed got into the back. Rourke turned and shot a final wave to the men he'd trained.

They didn't see it. Already, they were clambering back up the embankment, toward the mountains, to attempt to intercept the men who had been destined to receive and transfer the shipment of raw opium.

The pilot swung the helicopter out over the gorge and flew parallel to the mountain road for several kilometers, then started climbing. Rourke turned to look behind him, feeling at the same moment, Muhammed's hand on his shoulder. "We are flying toward the Khyber Pass—it is not far. One of our border outposts was making its regular transmission, then suddenly the radio went silent. We want to be sure it is only some sort of equipment failure."

"Fine," Rourke said, nodding, but disinterested. He stared out the bubble dome and down to the valley floor thousands of feet below. After another moment, Muhammed said, "Tell me—I have read your file—but how does a man become a weapons expert, a survival expert, making a living out of teaching counter-terrorist techniques?"

"You read the file," Rourke said, chewing the stump of cigar between his teeth. "Like it says, I did counter-terrorist work for the CIA." His eyes crinkled into a smile—he'd actually been a field case officer in the Covert Operations Section. "Weapons," he went on, "were just a natural part of that—I've always been good with guns, ever since I was a kid. Hunted a lot, liked the woods, back-country camping. Sort of led me into survivalism. *And* I read the newspapers—scared hell out of me, too. So I learned everything I could about survival. I was on a job like this once, in Latin America," he said, finding himself shouting over the whir of the chopper blades. "Anyway," he went on, holding the cigar butt in his fingers and staring at it as he spoke, "those were my wilder days—back with the Company. With a bunch of anti-Communist partisans, I got ambushed. My right leg got shot up. Everybody else was killed. I was left for dead. I had a .45, an M-16 and a bayonet—no food, nothing in the way of medical supplies except some antibiotics. I couldn't get out of the jungle for six weeks. Then, when I did, the Communists had already taken over the country and I had to steal a boat—spent ten days in open water before I hit the Florida Keys. I was dehydrated, infected, sunburned and had about everything wrong with me except athlete's foot."

"Athlete's foot?" Muhammed asked, "This is a —"

"You know—between your toes," Rourke laughed.

"Ah, yes, we call it by another name."

"Yeah, well," Rourke continued, "but in spite of it all, I survived. Pretty proud of myself, I was. I'd learned a whole hell of a lot—particularly how much I didn't know. Went back to reading everything I could, going to every lecture I could, sorting through all the gimmickry and gadgets. There's more stuff to learn every day."

"But what is the purpose to it all?" Muhammed said. "Learning for itself is a noble purpose, to be sure, but—"

"Naw—it's a lot more practical than that," Rourke said, lighting the cigar again and getting an angry glare from the tomb-silent pilot sitting beside him. "There are enough loonies loose in the world today to screw up the planet so bad that survivalism training is going to be the only thing that'll keep people alive—maybe. What do you need—a runaway laboratory virus, a global economic collapse, a world crop failure?"

Below them now, Rourke saw the familiar craggy geography of the Khyber Pass, the historic gateway from Afghanistan to Pakistan. These days, he thought bitterly, Afghanistan was a Soviet satellite or the next best thing to one.

Muhammed leaned forward, speaking to the pilot, "Take the machine down—I want to see our border outpost from the air before we land."

Rourke reached into his borrowed jacket and took the tinted aviator sunglasses from their case and put them on, peering down toward the summit of the mountain.

"Ahh, Muhammed?"

"What is it, John Thomas?" Muhammed said.

Making a sharp, downward stab with his right thumb toward the Pakistani side of the pass, directly below them now, Rourke almost whispered, "Well, remember, I was talking about some of the reasons to study survivalism. I left out one—probably the most likely one as it looks from here."

The Pakistani officer edged forward in his seat, his face inches from Rourke's right shoulder. The smile which he usually wore degenerated into a blank stare, then froze into a grimace of fear. "Climb. Get us out of here!" Muhammed shouted.

Bending forward to light his cigar again, staring down as he did at the endless column of Soviet trucks, tanks, and armored personnel carriers rolling across the Khyber Pass below him, Rourke said, half to himself, "Yeah, Muhammed—one of the surefire best reasons for survivalism might be World War Three . . ."

Chapter Two

Corporal Ahmed Mahmude Shindi, his voice low, his speech clipped, rasped, "We cannot risk the radio. They may have all our communications channels monitored. You two," he whispered, gesturing to another corporal and a private, "must go back, back to the road. Follow it until you reach an outpost, and report what we have seen. Stop for nothing. Do whatever you must. But it is imperative that you get through."

The clouds which, throughout the day had been dark gray at the lower elevation, were now a black shroud through which the setting sun winked orange. Heavy snow, each flake the size of a large coin, began to fall.

Ahmed brushed the snow from his field glasses and hunched lower toward the barren wet ground as he edged up toward the rim of the gorge. A quick glance back over his left shoulder confirmed that his men were already setting out to alert military headquarters. Looking down into the dry rock bed several hundred yards beneath him, he saw Soviet troops half covered by the canvas shrouds of their stake trucks. And Soviet tanks, armored personnel carriers—all moving along the road below in a rapid single column. He refocused his binoculars back along the way from which the Soviets had come. He could see no end to the convoy.

The wind was gusting. The snow whirled around him like dust devils. Crawling back toward the small cave in the shelter of overhanging rocks under which his seven remaining men huddled, Ahmed's mind raced. Rourke who had taught him more than he had ever learned from anyone else about fighting and survival, had always repeated one admonition—to keep his head; regardless of the task, to do what you knew was the right thing in the right way.

"What," Ahmed asked himself, "is the right way of this?" Against the thousands of troops pouring along the road, down from Afghanistan, what could eight men hope to accomplish? He found himself shaking his head as, shivering with the cold and dampness now, he crawled under the lip of the low rock outcropping and into the small cave beside his men.

"What do we do, Corporal?"

It hardly mattered to Ahmed which of his men had asked the question—they all had the question in their minds. He said nothing for a moment—Rourke had been like that. The American had never talked just to talk. He had said little, in fact. But what the American had said when he did speak was always, worth remembering.

Slowly, Ahmed formulated the possible actions he could take. "There are thousands of Soviet troops coming down from the Khyber Pass—you have all seen this. We are eight men only. We cannot stop them. But if we withdraw and simply let them proceed, we will be failing our responsibilities as Pakistanis—as men. If we can do something that delays their invasion of our country by even so much as a single moment, we will have done something to help our people. We will have struck a blow. If we stay here, my friends, we will be safe, at least for the moment. If we fight—and we may achieve nothing—we will most surely die. I cannot make the decision for you. But I ... I will fight."

Ahmed leaned back against the cold rock of the cave wall and took a cigarette from his tunic. His wife had been telling him that smoking so was bad for him, and he had promised her to try to stop. Now, he had passed a sentence of death on himself. The smoking could no longer hurt him. It almost made him laugh. As he sucked the smoke deep into his lungs, he took a photograph, plastic covered, from his wallet. It almost made him cry.

He stared at the face of his wife, the smile in the eyes of the baby girl she had given him less than a year before. He stared at the photo as if somehow by looking at the picture he was communicating his thoughts to them. "I love you," he shouted but in silence. Not caring what his men saw, he touched his lips to the photo, then replaced it in his wallet.

The cigarette, burnt down to a tiny, glowing butt, became the focus of his attention. Staring at it, he said to his men, his voice cold like his feet, his hands, his back, "Who goes with me to fight?"

Ahmed stared into their faces. One by one, each nodded or gestured with a hand. Already, some of them were looking to their weapons.

"Come then," he said.

"Wait!" It was the young private who had spoken when Ahmed had first returned to the cave. "We should pray before we die."

Ahmed nodded, and the young private began. Ahmed's eyes flickered from one face to the other as each made his own peace. And then the prayer was over. Saying nothing, Ahmed started from the cave. The others followed him back into the swirling snow, the darkness, the wind and the cold.

They moved along the rim of the gorge. In less than an hour of numbing temperature and chill wind, exhaustion and total silence, they cut the road and reached a low rock ledge. Following it down, toward the roadside, Ahmed guessed that they were ten minutes ahead of the lead Soviet truck and the motorcycles just in front of it.

As they reached the road surface, Ahmed smiled—there were no tracks in the snow. The snow—he looked above him toward the clouded sky, watching the swirling mass of white coming down—was a blessing from Allah. The Russians could not use their helicopters or fighter planes this night.

He stopped by the side of the road and called his men to a halt. "We must go down the road along the side here. In that way, they will not see our tracks. Come." In single file, at some times climbing back up into the rocks, they walked along the roadside, going for perhaps a mile, before they halted once more.

"You four," he said, gesturing with his numbing left hand, "will stay here. The rest of us will move further down, then cross the road and retrace our steps along the opposite side. When the Russians come, open fire on the motorcycles with your submachine guns. Each grenadier will open fire on the nearest truck. The grenadier with me will use his last rounds on the outcroppings of rock above us here. If we can block the road with a rock slide, we will delay the Russians even more. You are good men," Ahmed said finally, then turned and started along the edge of the road.

With his three-man unit, he moved on several hundred yards, then hurriedly crossed the, road. Doubling back took longer than he had planned; there was little ground between the road and the yawning chasms below. At times he and his men were forced to crawl on their hands and knees through the snow to avoid slipping and falling to their deaths.

They finally stopped, parallel to the other four men, and just opposite them on the protected side of the road. Ahmed checked his watch. As if to confirm that the watch was keeping accurate time, he heard the rumbling of the trucks. Ahmed directed his men to conceal themselves on the edge of the road, behind the slight protection of a small spit of rock jutting out over the void.

Except for the rumbling of the trucks, all else was silence. The snowfall heightened the noise of the trucks. Perhaps the convoy was not so near, he thought. Ahmed glanced over the rock behind which he hid. He could see the headlamps of the slow-moving motorcycles, snow swirling in the probing fingers of light as they wove through the darkness. Ahmed had ridden a motorcycle many times, and for an instant was touched with compassion for the Russians aboard them. The road was icy now, and uneven to begin with. Maneuvering the cycles on such a night, mere inches at times from a thousand-foot drop, would be constant terror.

Ahmed could see the first of the motorcycles clearly now. One man riding, one man in the sidecar, their clothes covered with snow. He watched as the lead cyclist momentarily freed his heavily gloved fingers from the handlebars of the machine and brushed at the goggles covering his eyes.

Ahmed, bracing the H-K submachine gun against his shoulder, screamed, "Open fire!"

With his first burst, he shot the man riding in the sidecar rather than the cyclist.

The H-K 69's were already belching their 40-mm high-explosive charges. The first truck was less than a hundred yards away. As the grenade hit, the truck gushed into flame. Soviet troops, their uniforms afire, poured from the back of the vehicle. They fired at the flame-covered troops from each side of the road, gunning them down.

Another truck exploded a moment later, flames from the fireball licking out in the high wind, catching the tarp covering of the center truck. It, too, burst into flames.

Ahmed threw down his submachine gun, the weapon empty, his last magazine shot out. He snatched at the 9-mm pistol on his belt, shot out the first magazine, then reloaded and picked off more of the Russians as they scattered from their burning vehicles.

The ground below him shook, and Ahmed fell back, the pistol, only half empty, flying from his hands. Looking up—his right eye was blurred—he saw the Soviet tank pushing the burning trucks out of its way as it thundered down the road. He started shouting to the grenadier—but the man had already fired. The grenade bounced against the tank's armor and exploded. The Soviet giant was unaffected. "Russian armor," he muttered to himself. "The rocks!" he shouted to his grenadier.

As the grenadier started firing at the rock outcropping on the opposite side of the road, Ahmed reached into his left pocket, his frostbitten fingers touching the butt of the flare pistol which Rourke had given him. Stiffly, he crammed a cartridge into the chamber and set it to fire.

The rocks across the road were already crumbling under the impact of the grenades. Huge boulders crashed down and blocked the road bed.

The ground shook again, and Ahmed's ears rang. He bounced skyward and came down hard against the road surface. He twisted his head to see with his good eye—the pain almost made him pass out. The grenadier was gone—nowhere to be seen. Ahmed started to cough; thoughts of his wife and daughter merged with the terror of death that was sweeping over him. He looked up. A Soviet soldier was standing above him, a submachine gun in his raw, bare hands.

Ahmed raised Rourke's flare pistol and pulled the trigger just as the first of the Soviet trooper's bullets cut through him.

Ahmed wanted to die with his eyes closed, but he stared sightlessly up at the falling snow.

Chapter Three

"Mr. Ambassador, wake up sir, please!"

Stromberg rolled over. The weak-bulbed bedside lamp was on. He closed his eyes against the dim light. "What the hell are you doing here at—" Stromberg glanced at the watch on his nightstand—"at three in the morning? My God, man! Where's Mrs. Stromberg?"

"I knocked and she let me in, sir. When I sort of told her what was going on, she said to wake you myself—she was going to make some coffee for you. I said I could get someone from the staff, but—"

"Never mind that, Hensley! What the hell are you waking me up for, to begin with? You know I've got that trade conference tomorrow morning at nine—*this* morning!" Stromberg yawned, found his glasses and put them on, at the same time running his spatulate fingers through his thinning gray hair.

"Sir, it's an eyes-only message. You're going to have to decode it. It's direct from the president, not the secretary. But it's signed by him too, sir."

"Oh, hell," Stromberg groaned. "Probably forgot to send somebody an anniversary card or something."

"But, sir," the young cipher clerk insisted, "the code is Maximum Priority. You've got to read it now."

"Hensley," Stromberg said, trying to roll over between his blankets, then pushing himself into a sitting position. "You've got to learn one thing, young man. Nothing in the State Department ever happens that won't wait until morning. Well, I shouldn't say that," he added as he started to come awake. "There's only one reason they'd send a message like that, and that's imposs—" He reached over to the bedside table and grabbed a cigarette from a small jade box. Hensley lurched forward and lit it. "There's only one thing, as I said that—" He stared at the message. "Good God! Hensley, get my robe!"

Stromberg was halfway to the door before Hensley could intercept him, helping him on with his robe as the ambassador fumbled with the doorknob, then threw open the door to his private office.

Inside, Stromberg took the Andrew Wyeth painting from the wall behind his desk, then felt along the joint of the wall paneling. A piece of the paneling slid away, revealing a small wall safe.

"Sir," Hensley said. Then, clearing his throat, repeated himself, "Sir!"

"What is it, man?"

"I shouldn't be here when you go into that safe, sir—that's against security—"

"The hell with security, Hensley," Stromberg said.

There was a knock at the door.

"Come in!" Stromberg half-shouted.

"Coffee, darling—hot." Mrs. Stromberg was young—Stromberg couldn't help but be reminded of that as she entered the room. Hensley stared at her. Her robe was more revealing than Stromberg would have liked.

She started to leave the room, and Stromberg said, "No. Wait here."

He had the safe open, then sat down at his desk. Looking at Hensley, he said, "Let's see that message again."

"Here, sir," Hensley said. "Should I go now?"

"No—wait. Let's see what this sucker—sorry dear," he said absently to his wife, then, "Let's see what this is all about."

Stromberg's wife stood beside him, lighting another cigarette, then putting it between his lips as he worked at the tiny, gray canvas-bound code book. Stromberg could taste her lipstick on the cigarette filter.

He stopped halfway through the message. "Hensley, get the embassy security chief up here, pronto. You come back, too. On the way, go down to the code room and get Washington to retransmit this, to be sure. Verify that they haven't changed Sigma 9, RB 18 since the last time my book was updated."

"Should I say that, sir, I mean *en clair*?"

"Yes, Hensley. They can always change the code later." And as Hensley left the room, Stromberg muttered, "If there is a later—"

After several minutes he looked up from his desk, stared across the room and saw his wife sitting in the chair opposite his desk, smoking one of his cigarettes. She only smoked his cigarettes, never bought any of her own because she smoked so seldom. He had often wished he could control smoking the way she did—half a pack or a pack one day, nothing for several weeks, then a single cigarette. She had will power.

Stromberg looked across the message in his hands, saying, "I'll read this to you, Jane. If it's an error, it doesn't make any difference. We'll know that in a minute. If it's true—" he shrugged—"doesn't make much difference, either."

"Security will be miffed with you, George," she warned, smiling.

"Piss on security," he grunted. "Here—listen." Instruct you to advise Soviet Premier, formally, in person, following. Ongoing Soviet invasion of Pakistan begun zero eight forty-five Washington time must be halted immediately. Troops must be withdrawn to Afghani border. United States views Soviet aggression in Pakistan as gross violation of Geneva Accords and threat to United States security. STOP. Severe international repercussions will result. The possibility of United States and other NATO power armed intervention not ruled out. Word it tactfully but strongly, George. End it.' "

"My God," the woman whispered.

"It's signed by the president, Jane."

"Do you want me to pretend to be a secretary and call the premier for you?"

"What?" Stromberg said. "Oh, yeah—please. Good idea."

He stood and walked to the window, staring out onto the embassy grounds below. "This could mean a world war, Jane," he whispered. His breath clouded the window pane.

"I know, George." He heard her answer over the clicking of the telephone dial.

"No—wait," he said suddenly. "Hensley hasn't verified the Sigma 9, RB 18 code yet." But he knew the wait was a waste of time.

The message was correct.

Chapter Four

The tiny alcove in the antechambers of the premier's office was oppressive. Its cold, almost sterile stone seemed to close in on George Stromberg as he waited, pacing and smoking, looking for an ashtray.

He turned, hearing the premier's young male secretary reenter the room.

"The premier will see you now, Ambassador Stromberg."

"Thank you." Stromberg followed the secretary down the hallway, past the premier's formal office, then into another carpeted hall. They stopped before a small dark wooden door. The secretary knocked, then, without waiting for a reply opened the door and stepped aside for Stromberg to enter.

Stromberg waited until the secretary had gone to say anything—the premier rarely advertised the fact that he spoke excellent English.

"Mr. Stromberg, what an unexpected pleasure." Behind the desk, its green blotter beathed in yellow-tinged light, sat the premier.

"Good evening, sir," Stromberg said perfunctorily, then approached the desk.

He could see only the bottom half of the premier's face, the stubble showing that the man had not bothered shaving for Stromberg's unexpected visit. But was it unexpected, Stromberg wondered? If he had learned anything in three years of representing U.S. interests in Moscow, it was that every Russian politician was a consummate actor, and the premier was perhaps the best of all.

"Sit down, please, Mr. Stromberg. You must be tired."

"I am, sir," Stromberg said, sitting in the worn leather chair opposite the desk.

The yellow circle of light from the old gooseneck lamp on the premier's desk left the man's eyes in shadow. Stromberg was unable to read his face.

"And why have you come, Mr. Stromberg? An urgent message from your government?"

"I see no reason why we should mince words, sir," Stromberg said.

The premier, Stromberg decided, knew him well. The long, bony fingers of his left hand pushed a small glass ashtray into the pool of light and toward Stromberg. "Feel free to smoke, if you choose."

"Thank you, sir," Stromberg said, then fumbled out his cigarettes and the Dunhill lighter which Jane had given him on his last birthday. Suddenly, Stromberg felt afraid. Had it been his last birthday, hers, everyone's?

"Mr. Stromberg, since we are speaking plainly, I assume your president wishes to convey some message about our recent decision to protect the internal security of the people of Pakistan. And how is your president, by the way? I was, in all honesty, expecting a call from him directly. But ... I see this is not the case. Would that we could talk person-to-person as people think we do." He chuckled.

Stromberg watched the premier's mouth in the light. The lips set into a tight half-smile.

"A formal note signed by the president will arrive by courier later in the morning. However, the president wishes me to convey his best personal wishes, and that he is troubled by what he can only interpret as an act of aggression—not only against the autonomous government of the people of Pakistan, but against our mutual interest of world peace."

"It depends, Mr. Stromberg," the premier said. A match flashed in the darkness near his heavy brow, then a cloud of cigar smoke filtered into the light of the gooseneck lamp. "It depends upon how one interprets things. We *are* preserving peace."

"Mr. Premier," Stromberg said, clearing his throat, "you said we were speaking frankly. May I?"

"Certainly, Stromberg. We are old friendly adversaries. I sent your daughter a fur ski jacket for her eleventh birthday, remember?"

"Yes, sir—she still wears it often. In fact, she wanted me to thank you personally for the porcelain doll you sent."

"I mean no harm to *you*," the premier whispered, "nor to your wife and daughter, Stromberg. So tell me—the truth."

"Sir," Stromberg said, leaning forward in his chair, desperately trying to glimpse the premier's eyes, "my president's message was that if Soviet forces are not withdrawn from Pakistan to beyond the border with Afghanistan, there could be severe international repercussions, possible military intervention in Pakistan by U.S. and NATO forces."

"And you feel, Stromberg," the premier said, his voice tired-sounding, "that your president is talking about what you would call World War Three, no?"

"Sir, the president's message said nothing of global war."

"But total war was between the lines, was it not?"

Stromberg said nothing, and the premier went on. "I will speak frankly with you. It is hard, your not being Russian to understand us. We think in two different languages. In two different ways. You cannot think in the manner that we do, and we cannot think as you do. I appreciate your trying to learn our language. We see our movement into Pakistan as the only way to make our posture in Afghanistan tenable."

"As you, sir, must believe me," Stromberg said, lighting another cigarette, "when I tell you that a military response is our only tenable reply to your move."

"I know this, and for this reason I am sitting here with you at an unholy hour! I do not want a war with the United States. I have never wished this. But you must believe what I am about to tell you. In some ways it is highly secret, but you must know it if you are to prevent a war.

"The American press," the premier went on, "has called Afghanistan a Soviet Viet Nam. It is. But we cannot afford to withdraw from Afghanistan. The United States does not border Viet Nam—it is oceans and thousands of kilometers away. We do border Afghanistan. Some of our most important research facilities are near it. Today, the Moslem populations of our own territories grow restless. Were something the likes of which your government allowed to transpire in Iran to have taken place in Afghanistan, it could have spread into our borders. Guns and propaganda and fighting men are entering Afghanistan through Pakistan. This must stop. No one else in the world has decided to stop it, so we must."

"But, sir, the entry into Afghanistan is still the subject—"

"Of much debate, yes I know. I am tired of debate. Russian soldiers are dying in Afghanistan. Debate does not bring them back to life! If we were to pull out of Afghanistan, the Moslem peoples in the Soviet Union would view this as a sign of weakness and we might well have open revolt. For a variety of reasons, this could not be tolerated. You know this. It is common knowledge that our primary particle beam weapon research facilities are in an area close to Afghanistan and peopled largely by Moslems. We are advanced—vastly. No—the word is superior. We are superior to you in this field. We are—and you must believe this—at the stage where our particle beam weapons can be deployed terrestrially. I am not talking about laser-equipped hunter-killer satellites at thirty thousand meters overhead or some such. I am talking about cannon-like particle beam weapons which can destroy any American missiles or bombs before they can deliver their weapons and warheads. We are militarily superior."

"We are aware of Soviet strides in particle beam weaponry," Stromberg said. "The United States has made similar strides, in some instances along parallel lines."

"We know what you have and what you don't have," the premier said, almost bored. "Ask anyone who has the better of intelligence services. We do. The world knows this. And you must now believe me. This is why we have for so long been sincerely interested in strategic arms limitation talks—to limit nuclear weapons. We can survive with what we have, and still be victorious if need be. But I am not saying this as a threat."

"Then why *are* you telling me this, sir?"

"It is simple," the premier answered slowly. "We do not wish the destruction of the world. There. That is something your president can understand, something on which we are both agreed. We will not withdraw our troops from Pakistan until significant border regions of that nation are totally under Soviet control. We will then leave a residual peace-keeping force and conclude prosecution of the matter in Afghanistan. Within perhaps a few months, at most a few years, Soviet troops will be withdrawn from Pakistan. This, I pledge. But not before." He drummed his right fist down hard on the desk.

Stromberg watched the hand. His own father had been a roofer before forming his own construction business and rising in society. Stromberg remembered his father's hands—the huge knuckles. The premier had been a roofer as a young man—had Stromberg not already known that, the massive, raw-boned knuckles would have told him. "The United States certainly does not wish a war with the

Soviet Union or any other power, yet we must again insist on the sovereignty of Pakistan."

"Mr. Stromberg," the premier said, "you are an ambassador—you are not paid to say what you think. I am a premier—I am paid to say what I think." He paused. Then: "I do not think the United States will risk a world war over Pakistan. You are bluffing—that is the expression, yes?"

Stromberg nodded.

"Bluffing, then. You have in the past—a great deal. You will again. We will sometimes acquiesce to your bluffing simply to avoid protracted difficulties. But this time, the Soviet Union will not back down. If the president chooses to make his ultimatum public, he will only lose face in the world community. NATO will not back you—of this, I am sure. The Warsaw Pact Nations can easily defeat even the most innovative NATO strategy in Europe. You are hopelessly outnumbered, my friend. If your president is foolish enough to begin a war with us, he will not win. He will be remembered as the destroyer of the United States, not its avenging savior. Perhaps he will be remembered as the destroyer of the world—if there is anyone left to remember him."

"You would risk that, Mr. Premier?" Stromberg said, incredulous.

"I speak of the welfare of my nation. A man must be willing to risk all for a cause he feels is just. Do you think this is only the prerogative of the West, my friend Stromberg? If you do, then you understand us less than I had thought."

"What can—" Stromberg stammered.

"Go and tell these things to your president, convince him of my sincerity and my earnest wish for peace. Do not trouble yourself to return here with the formal note. Your assistants can handle that. My formal reply shall be ready for return to your president by then. Now go." Stromberg started to stand up, but then the premier said, "A bit of advice to you. I like to think that as well as possible we have become something of friends over these three years since your posting here. Stay in the Soviet Union—you will be safe. At least, if you cannot, keep your wife and daughter safe here. I will guard them as if they were my family. Moscow is impervious to attack. It will be—in that eventuality—the safest place on earth for them."

Stromberg looked into the darkness as he stood before the premier's desk. "I used to have nightmares about something like this."

The premier whispered, so softly that the American ambassador could barely make out the words: "I still do."

Chapter Five

Sarah Rourke rolled over and opened her eyes, leaned toward the bedside lamp, and squinted as she pulled the chain for the light. Looking away from the glare as much as she could, she studied the digital alarm clock beside the bed—Michael would be late for kindergarten. She felt behind the clock. The alarm had been pushed off.

She sat bolt upright in bed, pushing her shoulder-length brown hair back from her face. She had watched the network news the previous evening, then had a hard time getting to sleep afterward. As she pulled away the covers and edged her feet out of the bed, she wondered if John had made it out of Pakistan before the Russians had entered the country. Gingerly, she tested the rug with her toes until she found her slippers, then slipped her feet into them and stood up.

Her pale blue nightgown brushed at her ankles as she reached for the robe on the chair beside the bed and slipped it on.

"Michael!" she called from her door, "get up for school. Mommy overslept. Come on. You too, Ann," she called to their four-year-old daughter.

"I'll get Ann, Mom," Michael shouted back.

"All right. I'll make breakfast. You can eat at school today. No time for me to make your lunch."

She glanced into Michael's room first. His was across the hall from her own. And then into Ann's room before she started toward the head of the stairs.

She stopped. She'd thought she smelled cigar smoke, but supposed it was only her imagination—despite herself she'd been thinking of John all night. But as she stood there at the head of the stairs, she could smell it now quite distinctly. She rubbed her eyes and peered over the bannister into the living room below. Someone was in the easy chair by the fireplace—and there was a fire going.

Over the mantel, the brass brackets for the shotgun which John had insisted she keep there were empty. "My God," she started to say, her hazel eyes staring straight at the back of the head that was half visible above the chair's headrest.

"You can relax, Sarah."

He stood and looked up at her, the shotgun and an old rag in his hands. It was John, and for an instant she wasn't sure she was glad. If it had been a prowler, she would have known how to react. But with her husband, she no longer did.

"Daddy!" It was Michael screaming and running past her, taking the steps down two at a time; then Ann was racing past her too, "Daddy! Daddy!"

Sarah Rourke turned and walked back down the hallway. He'd been cleaning the shotgun. His obsession, she realized, with guns and death and violence hadn't gone away. Her stomach was churning. She stumbled into the bathroom. Obsession. She looked into the mirror, studied her face a moment, touched her right hand to her hair, realizing that she was like him—obsessed.

*****

John Rourke pulled his wife's '78 Ford wagon to a halt on the gravel driveway in front of the house. He could see Sarah waiting for him in the doorway—blue jeans with a few smears of paint on them, a T-shirt with one of his own plaid flannel shirts over it. Her hair was loose at her shoulders, a cup of coffee steamed in her hands, and her hazel eyes stared over it at him.

"Well," he began, across the driveway from her, "I got the kids to school—they weren't too late."

"Have to kill anybody along the way, John?" Without waiting for an answer, she turned and walked back inside the house.

As Rourke pulled his leather jacket shut against the cold, he felt the stainless Detonics .45 in his hip pocket. He'd left its mate and double shoulder rig in the house, and realized that she'd seen it.

"Shit," he muttered to himself, then walked across the gravel and up the three steps and onto the long riverboat front porch, then into the high-ceilinged old house. "Where are you?" he half-shouted.

"In the kitchen—making your breakfast," Sarah called back. He tossed his jacket on the coat tree and walked the length of the hallway to the end, then turned into the kitchen.

"You finished stripping the wainscoting? It looks good that way," Rourke said, sitting down in front of the steaming mug of coffee that waited for him on the trestle table.

"It was a lot of work," she said, still facing away from him, standing by the electric stove. "The woodwork, I mean," she added, her voice low.

"How are the kids?" he said.

"Didn't you ask them?" She turned toward him and put a plate before him— a small steak, two eggs, hash brown potatoes and toast.

"I didn't expect this," he said.

"Didn't you ask them—the children?" she repeated.

"Yeah," he said, a forkful of egg and potato poised in front of his mouth. "I asked them—all they said was they missed me. Said you missed me too," he added.

"Well—they do. I do, but that doesn't change anything." Sipping at her coffee, she said, "I was worried you hadn't gotten out of Pakistan in time. The Russians and everything. I thought you were supposed to be in Canada for that seminar on—what is it?"

"Hyperthermia," Rourke said. "Field recognition and treatment of hyperthermia—a lot of interest in that these days."

"Why didn't you become a doctor after medical school? You're crazy."

"Dammit, Sarah," Rourke said.

"Well, why didn't you? You went to college, took pre-med, went to medical school, then you quit and went into the CIA. You're an idiot."

Rourke threw his fork down on the plate, then stood and walked to the window looking out onto the enclosed back porch. "What? You want the same argument we had last time?"

"No," she said quietly. "I just want different answers."

"I like what I'm doing."

"Killing people?"

Rourke turned and glared at her, realizing he still had the gun in his pocket. Weighing it in his hand a moment, he set it on top of the refrigerator and sat down again.

"Answer me. Do you really enjoy violence?"

Biting down hard on a piece of toast, he said quietly, "I'll tell you one more time. I enjoy working with police and military people. Training them how to stay alive. If staying alive entails killing someone else, then, okay—it does. I didn't make the world. Somebody has to teach people how to stay alive in it. I know all there is to know about terrorism, brushfire wars—but it's more than that. Just the day-to-day business of staying alive would kill most people if they found themselves in the wilderness, the desert . . . if they lost their modern technology in a flood or a quake. Most people—"

"Like me?" she said defensively.

"Yes. Yes, like you or anybody else. Do you know anything about edible plants? Ever skin down a snake then worry about whether you'd gotten all the poison out because if you didn't eat it you'd starve to death? No. But I have."

"What do you want, a medal? I don't mind that part of it—but why is it always tied to death? I bet you're hoping the Russians go straight on through Pakistan and we go to war with them. Then everybody'd have to tell you you were right." Then, deepening her voice and frowning, she shouted, "Plan now for death and destruction—read the collected works of J.T. Rourke, noted survivalist and weapons expert. That's right, ladies and gentlemen, he can tell you how to survive war, famine, death—and, if you act now, he'll even throw in pestilence at no extra charge."

"Hell, lady," Rourke said, downing his coffee. "If I really thought you believed that, I'd give up on this whole damned thing between us."

"What? Divorce instead of the separation we have now?"

Rourke stood, walked around the table and put his hand on her shoulder, felt her touch her face against his hand, then felt her lips touch his fingers.

"Why do we fight?" she whispered.

"Because we love each other. Otherwise, we'd have given up a long time ago."

"On that," she said, "I'll admit you're right."

Rourke dropped to his knees beside her chair and wrapped his arms around her, feeling her body pressing against him. They stayed that way for a long time.

When he sat down again his coffee was cold and so was the food.

"I'll make some more coffee—would you like some more coffee?" she said, standing across the room by the stove.

"Yes, I'd like some more coffee." He smiled, and she laughed. While the fresh pot brewed, he followed her into her studio across the hall. "What's the latest book?" he asked, leaning over the slanted drawing table by the window.

"I don't have a title for it yet," she said, leaning over with him to look at the drawings. "Do you like them?"

"A snow leopard?" he said, pointing to one of the loose drawings at the top of the table. It was part of a composite. She had always made drawings and backgrounds separately, then combined them. It was a slow process, but her illustrations for the children's books which she also wrote had received considerable critical acclaim over the years.

"Yes," she said, her voice soft and girlish as she looked at the picture he held. "It's about a snow leopard. They're arboreal—hardly ever come down from the trees. This one has to. He's exploring a new world that's been right under his own world all his life."

Rourke put his arms around her. "What about the coffee?" she asked, pushing her hands against his chest.

"Pull the plug."

"Okay."

Hand-in-hand, they went back to the kitchen for a moment while she unplugged the electric coffee pot. Then the two of them went back down the hall and up the stairs to the second floor, into the bedroom.

Sun was streaming through the sheer curtains on the broad-paned windows. Rourke folded Sarah into his arms. His hands pressed tight against her back and her rear end. Her arms twined around his neck. She leaned up toward him and he kissed her lips, gently, then with greater force as her hands caressed his face. His hands slowly explored the familiar curves of her body.

They undressed each other by the windows. She smiled, almost blushing, as he stripped away her bra. They stood naked for a moment, arms about each other, watching the autumn-like landscape on the other side of the glass. Their land stretched for miles into the woods, whose deciduous and coniferous trees were untouched, save for the yearly Christmas tree they always cut and a few trees felled for wood to stoke the house's several fireplaces.

"In Pakistan, up in the mountains," Rourke whispered, "it's winter."

She touched her fingers to his lips and he pushed them away, kissing her again, then walking with her the few short steps to the unmade bed.

They sat on the edge of the bed while she told him what Michael and Ann had been doing since the last time he had come to see them all—just before he left for Pakistan. Then, naturally and easily, they fell back onto the bed, slipped under the sheet, warming each other for a while as their hands touched each other's bodies.

Rourke felt her hands slip between his thighs. His own hands touched her breasts, her thighs, then he moved over her, slipping between her thighs. Her back arched, her stomach pressing up against him. His lips touched her neck, her ear, her cheek, and as their mouths touched, their tongues touched also, the tip of hers at once exploring and inviting his. Her hands were guiding him and he moved against her, the moisture and heat of her, the twitching of her small muscles around him making him push all the more deeply into her.

Her breaths were short and erratic as she moved under him, her eyes closed, the lids fluttering as he watched them, sunlight through the curtains splashing across the face he knew so well . . .

*****

They walked in the woods, both of them having showered together after they'd left the bed. Rourke wore jeans and boots and a pale blue shirt. His leather coat was open. Sarah's arm wrapped around his waist and under her coat. She shivered a little as they stepped into a small clearing a few hundred yards from the old house.

"Why did you come back, John?" she whispered, quietly.

"To see if we could patch things up. I don't care whether you think what I'm doing is right or wrong. But I want to be with you—you and the kids."

"But what *about* the children?" she said. "I don't want them growing up with the idea that death and violence are just normal—like you feel. Maybe you *are* right—I'll give you that. Maybe I'm so wrong that I'm a fool. But if everyone does nothing but prepare for the destruction of civilization, there won't be any civilization left to be destroyed. Do you know what I mean?"

"If the world is going to end, you'd rather not know about it?"

"Maybe. Maybe it's something like that. I don't want Michael and Ann growing up with guns and violence—there are other things. You, of all people, should know that. But you ignore it."

Rourke walked away from her and sat on a deadfall log in the middle of the clearing. In a moment she was standing beside him, her hands resting on his shoulders. "After all these years you still don't understand what I'm doing," he said. "You should come up to the retreat. Maybe you'd understand it better then."

"What do you mean?"

"All the money I've poured into the retreat over the last few years—you never once would go there. It's not an arsenal. It's a part of civilization, a protected piece. That's why I put it where I did—up in the mountains. That's why you can only get there by horse or motorbike—in good weather, with a four by four truck."

Sitting down beside him, she said, "All right. Tell me about the retreat."

Rourke looked at her, then said, "Okay. I'll tell you about it. You never wanted to know before." He sighed. "It was a cave to begin with. I bought the piece of the mountain first, then sealed off the cave completely—waterproofed it, everything. Using the natural configuration of the rocks, I built a second home there—for all of us. A place we could use when we wanted just to get away from things. And a place that, if everything fell apart, we could go to and still live like human beings. I turned the mouth of the cave into a long hallway. At the end of it is the great room—the ceiling must be thirty feet high and its natural rock. It's huge. It's the library, living room, recreation room—it's just where you live. Opening off that are three smaller rooms that are bedrooms. Another room with a full kitchen. Baths, everything. The electrical power comes from an underground spring that runs the generators I installed. Heating is electric—with the rock and the high ceilings you never need cooling."

"It sounds like something from a science fiction movie."

"Maybe," Rourke said. "But it's nice—beautiful, comfortable, secure. The air that comes into the place is all filtered and scrubbed. Far in the back I built a humidified greenhouse that uses electric plant lights—those things last almost forever. Its self-contained, an environment within an environment. Books, music, videotape equipment, enough rations for the four of us for a couple of years. I even laid up a supply of booze. It's *not* an arsenal. Most of my guns I have with me all the time. I keep a few there. A lot of ammunition there. But that's just for security if necessary, and for hunting, not for a war."

"But if there were a collapse, John, wouldn't your retreat be discovered? I mean, how can you keep something like that hidden?"

"*Our* retreat, Sarah," Rourke said. "And it wouldn't be discovered. From the outside it looks like just granite outcropping of the mountain. The entrance is completely concealed. Nobody'd find it unless they knew it was there and made an organized search of the whole area to find the entrance. It's even got an emergency escape exit along the stream that powers the place. And the water is fresh. I've got a filtering system to use if necessary, but the water apparently stays deep underground for a long time. It's clearer and sweeter than anything you've ever drunk. The temperature of the water is so cold, the spring might start off up by-Canada. There's no way to tell."

She turned her face to his and said abruptly, "Why aren't you in Canada for your lecture, John?"

"Simple," he said, his voice low, his eyes staring down at the ground between his boots. "I was in a helicopter with my Pakistani liaison officer. On the way out we saw the first prong of the Soviet invasion from the air. I've still got plenty of contacts with CIA and State. If the Russians don't pull out of Pakistan, we're going in with troops to push them out. And you know what that could start."

"God, John, no. No one would be senseless enough to start a world war. I just can't believe that."

"Well," Rourke said, "I hope you're right. In case you aren't, though, I wanted to try to persuade you to come to the retreat with the kids—stay with me there until this thing all blows over, or—"

She cut him off. "Or until the war starts and we can't leave."

"Something like that," he said, not looking at her.

"You go to Canada," she whispered. "And when you come back, let's try to start over again. Maybe we'll even visit your—*our*—retreat. How long will you be gone?"

"It's three days—with travel, make it four. I don't *have* to go."

"Yes, you do. If I want to get myself psyched up for trying again, you've got to. Can you stay the night and leave in the morning?"

"Do you want me to?"

"Yes," Sarah said, her voice a whisper.

Chapter Six

"Commanche Nine holding at Fail Safe point, sir," the young airman droned, still studying the control panel before him. The captain behind him did not indicate whether he had heard him, but continued walking along the rank of thirty-six consoles on the mezzanine overlooking the Sioux Mountain Strategic Air Command Global Layout. The lights of the console blinked on and off in various colors, indicating the positions and statuses of flights. Many of the lights were glowing amber; those flights were all within a few air miles of the Soviet mainland, and the amber color indicated they were armed with nuclear warheads and holding at the Fail Safe point—poised to penetrate Soviet defenses, armed and ready, awaiting a digitally coded attack order. Once that was issued, only a specific, complex recall code could be issued to make the bombers pull out.

At the end of the rank of consoles and blue-clad airmen monitoring them, the captain turned a corner and moved along the catwalk to the other side of the mammoth, amphitheater-like room. On this side, there was a nearly identical row of airmen, with nearly identical consoles. The map on the far wall of this room was nearly identical to the one on the other, but the lights were in different patterns and of different colors.

Here, most of the lights were navy blue—Soviet Ilyushin 28 and Mya-sishchev 500 bombers holding on their Fail Safe points—just a respectable distance outside the continental United States.

Lights changed, as the captain strolled past the map, but the numbers of them did not. There were quite a few more blue lights on this board than there were amber lights on the opposite board. The thought worried the captain slightly, and he made the decision that he should alert his superior to the numbers game scoring on the twin boards.

He picked up the receiver of the white phone nearest him, dialed the code, and waited.

*****

"You must go, sweetheart. Just a precaution, but a president is human, too. How can I function at my best if I'm worried about your safety and the safety of the children?" He smiled at her, not the smile he had used on election night, nor the smile he used at press conferences when one of the network reporters asked an awkward question—but the smile he saved for her and the children. As he put his arms around her, he reflected that it was likely his only real smile. There was little else to smile about these days.

"But, Andrew," she whispered, her cheek resting against the front of his blue three-piece suit, "why can't you go with us? You can run things just as well from Mt. Lincoln as you can from here. You've told me that yourself."

"Marilyn," he whispered, trying not to sound as concerned as he felt, "If the president were to go to his war retreat, it would look like we expected a war—and that might help to bring one about. Unless we were holding an exercise—which we aren't—I simply cannot go there. The people, would think war was imminent if I did."

"But isn't it, Andrew? The papers, the communiqués from Ambassador Stromberg? He's been back and forth to Russia twice in as many days."

"I know, darling. The premier is running a bluff. That particle beam weapon he talks about is still only experimental. If Moscow were ringed with operational PB devices, we'd know about it. Unfortunately, the papers, TV—they just don't believe we're telling them the truth, that the Soviets are running the risk of a U.S. retaliation. The premier is simply refusing to admit the fact that we're still militarily superior. He's running a bluff, and if I have to, I'll call it. But I want to save his credibility, as well—if I can, if he'll let me. I know the problems he faces in his own leadership in the Kremlin. I'll be on the hot line with him soon. We'll work it out. Remember, darling, the premier is no amateur. He's a reasonable man, a seasoned politician. We'll talk like reasonable men."

The president walked beside his wife down the hall and past the Oval Office to the narrow flight of stone steps leading to the driveway abutting the living quarters of the White House. The children were all waiting there. Andrew, Jr., seventeen; Louise, fourteen—named after her maternal grandmother—and Bobby, eight.

"Hey, Daddy!" Bobby shouted, running up to the president, a toy space ship in his hands, its laser cannons blasting.

The president bent down and swept the boy up into his arms. "And how are you, spaceman? What's the latest word from Alpha Centuri?"

"Oh, Daddy—I'm just playin'."

"Oh, okay," the president said. "How about giving the president a kiss—that's an order from the commander-in-chief of the space fleet."

The boy wrapped his arms around his father's neck. The president's eyes met his wife's for a brief moment as he bent to set the boy down.

"I want you to take care of your mother, Bob. You know she doesn't like helicopter rides. Oh, and I got Lieutenant Brightston to promise to haul out any videotape you want tonight and run it on the big screen at the mountain—so don't let him forget."

"Gotcha," the boy said, reaching up for a quick kiss, then running off toward his older brother and sister who were standing by the curb.

Out of the corner of his eye, the president saw his chief of staff, Paul Dorian, walking briskly down the steps, right hand raised discreetly, eyes boring toward him. "You go ahead, Marilyn," the president said, then waited, his shoulders hunched against the cold for Dorian to join him.

"What is it, Paul?"

"The full alert is in effect, sir. All standbys are cancelled—everything. Word from SAC Headquarters at Sioux Mountain is that the Russians are doing the same. CIA confirms that. So does Air Force intelligence, everything."

"The hot line?"

"Ready when you are, sir. The premier is available."

"Good," the president said, but the word soured in his mouth. "Oh, Paul?"

"Yes, Mr. President," Dorian said.

"Let's go ahead with that drill on the Eden Project thing—just in case."

The president studied the hard set Paul Dorian's eyes took. Mention of the Eden Project worried Dorian. As the president started toward his wife and children, to take the short walk to the White House lawn where his personal helicopter awaited, he thought, "All well and good." It was about time Paul Dorian started to worry.

Chapter Seven

Elizabeth Jordan brushed a wisp of blonde hair back from her forehead and tucked it under the thin wire band of her headset, then tapped out a response to Yuri Borstoi, who was on the other end of the hot line.

"Yuri, word is that the president will be on the line soon. What do you think on your end? Liz."

She waited as the satellite hook-up carried her message and as Yuri—the man she had known by satellite for three years—formed an answer. Like herself, Yuri was unmarried. At first jokingly, but in the last few months quite seriously, they had talked about meeting someday. The hot line was always kept open, testing and retesting that the vital link between East and West remained operational. And, when formal testing was not run, Administration almost encouraged a constant chatter along the line, to make sure it was in a constant state of readiness.

She had never heard Yuri's voice, but imagined what it was like. She had never seen his face, but they had described themselves to each other, and she had a fair enough idea of his looks. Now, as she waited for his reply, she tried to picture him. It was easy. His face was thin. He had said that he was a student nights at a Polytechnic Institute with a name she could not pronounce and that he didn't get enough sleep so there were dark circles under his eyes. His hair was black and straight. He was twenty-four—a year younger than she was. He had said his eyes were brown.

"Liz," the message began, "I too am worried. Reasonable men—I should not say this—can do unreasonable things. The premier will be coming on in a— must go. I love you."

He hadn't even had time for his signature. As the line went dead—the President and the Premier would be talking now—she realized too that it was the first time he had said, "I love you."

Chapter Eight

"I've read all the books and articles you put out, John. Fascinating stuff. The thing on hyperthermia should save a few lives, I'd say."

"That's the idea, Major," Rourke said, slumping back into the overstuffed chair. "It was nice of you to invite me to your home, by the way."

"Stranger in a strange country, and all that. Anyway, I had an ulterior motive," the Royal Canadian Mounted Police inspector said, smiling and handing Rourke a drink.

Rourke took the whiskey and sipped at it, then said, "And what was your ulterior motive?"

"As you probably know, John—It's not much of a secret—our services here are looking into quite a number of modern small arms for the military. Made me give some thought to weaponry for our specialized teams in RCMP. I know survival isn't your only thing. You know weapons too. Thought I might pry a few opinions from you while I ply you with some whiskey and my wife's home cooking."

"Ply away," Rourke said, smiling.

"Your mind is somewhere else, isn't it? That snowstorm sort of put the squeeze on your plans to fly out tonight. But the meteorology people are saying everything will be clear by midday tomorrow. Tonight, just take it easy."

"I'm worried about my family—all this war talk."

"Just talk, I think. I hope," the Canadian said brightly.

"Change of subject," Rourke said, raising his voice, slapping both knees. "Now, what do you want to know?"

"Well," the inspector said, touching his left hand to his small moustache, "when you're not teaching survivalism, but instead working with counter-terrorist weapons, what do you use?"

"You mean, which guns do I like best for myself—or which would I recommend for you?"

"I've read your recommendations on various things more often than I can remember, John. But what about you? What do you use?"

"All right," Rourke said, standing and walking toward the small library bar. Leaning against it, he said, "Short and sweet, then—I can smell dinner. I've got a lot of guns and knives and other stuff—but the things I really bank on are just a few. I always carry these." He spread his coat open, revealing the twin stainless steel Detonics .45s in their Alessi shoulder holsters. "Best automatic I know, bar none—when you consider effectiveness of the round they throw, reliability, and concealment characteristics. The stainless steel they use is the best quality. I almost never get the time to clean these things, and there isn't a spot of rust or corrosion. They work every time, and you can interchange the standard government model magazines, the whole bit."

"What else?" the major said.

"What else?" Rourke repeated. "When I'm in the field, I've got this Metalifed six-inch Python, had the barrel Mag-Na-Ported, got a set of .22 Long Rifle conversion chambers, and a barrel liner for it from Harry Owens—good for everything that way from a small bear in a pinch to a squirrel for the pot. Sometimes I use a Metalifed Colt Lawman snubby, too—when I want a third gun that I can conceal."

Rourke paused and lit his cigar, and as he started to speak, he heard the inspector's wife coming.

"I think you gentlemen might want to listen to the radio," she said, her voice subdued.

Without saying anything else, the attractive, middle-aged woman walked over to a corner of the built-in bookcases beyond the bar and clicked on the radio in the stereo. ". . . told that informed sources indicate the U.S. president and the Soviet premier have just completed a lengthy conversation, and that nothing has been resolved. An anonymous high- ranking military source at the Pentagon in Washington indicates U.S. Long Range Strike Force elements—a mobile military unit comprised of persons from all U.S. services analogous to our Special Commandoes—are at this moment being air-lifted toward Pakistan. Official Washington has been unavailable to confirm or deny this report. We now rejoin our regularly scheduled programming. More bulletins will be forthcoming as information becomes available." The inspector's wife clicked off the set.

"That's Roger Carrigborne," the major said, mechanically, tossing down his drink. "Fine chap—one of the best of the reporters—"

"I gotta get out of here," Rourke said, hammering down his half-emptied drink on the bar and spilling whiskey.

Chapter Nine

"My brother," the young soldier said, rubbing his hands to warm them, "has an easy job. He talks with this American girl on the satellite link between Moscow and Washington. That is all Yuri does. He even tells me he has fallen in love with her—though he never met her. He is warm. I am cold. He talks with American girls—I guard empty trucks on a mountain pass in Pakistan. He sits on a chair—I stand in the snow. This is not right."

"You talk too much," his sergeant said. The older man leaned against the fender of the nearest truck. "Ivan, I tell you the truth, the Americans may come and fight us. Some of our officers were speaking of this a few minutes ago."

"Good," Ivan said. "At least it would give me something to do instead of standing here, freezing, holding this damned rifle."

"I was sixteen and holding a rifle—with no bullets—at the siege of Stalingrad. Do not complain, young one," the sergeant said, his voice almost a whisper. "It was cold then, too, and I had holes in my boots. This night, I have bullets in my rifle and no holes in my boots. Things are better."

"Why are we here, Sergeant?" the soldier said, his voice trembling with the cold.

"We are Russians—that is why we are here. Tell me, Ivan Meliscovitch, do you and your brother who leads the easy life have a mother, or a sister?"

"Two sisters, Comrade Sergeant. Our mother is dead."

"Then you fight here for your sisters," the sergeant said. "Do not fight a war because you are trying to protect something you do not understand—politics, speeches. Fight to protect something you do understand and you will be stronger, fight harder. Hold on to life and be a brave man. I have three grandsons—younger than you. I fight for them. Years ago, I fought for my wife. But I cannot do that anymore." The sergeant's voice broke then, and he turned away and coughed.

The young soldier, Ivan, cleared his throat and started to speak. "Comrade Sergeant, I am sorry." The last word caught in his throat as a bright red flower of blood sparkled suddenly across the bridge of his nose and he crumpled back against the truck, the Kalashnikov pattern assault rifle falling from his gloved fingers.

The sergeant dropped flat down into the snow and rolled under the truck, glancing back and reaching out toward the dead boy—confirming that for himself—then slid under the belly of the truck, shouting, "We are under attack!"

There had been no sound of the shot. Was it a sniper with a silencer?

As the sergeant slid from under the truck, his long great coat was white with the snow. He scrambled to his feet. His knees ached with the cold. He ran in a low crouch toward the main body of his fellow soldiers. Already, as he ran, he heard sounds from the camps—shouts, rapidly barked commands, gunfire. "Fools!" the Sergeant thought. "Who are they shooting at?" He turned his head to glance back into the darkness from which the bullet that had killed Ivan Meliscovitch had come. The sergeant could see nothing.

He started to fall. As he went down he thought he had tripped on something in the snow, but when he tried to stand up, there was fire in his left ribcage. He touched his gloved right hand across his body to his coat, and his glove came back dark with blood. The sergeant pushed himself to his feet, lurched forward, two steps, then three, then fell again. A loud cry came from deep in his chest as his face pushed down against the wet snow: "Natalia!" The sergeant closed his eyes . . .

*****

The truck bounced hard on the rutted, snow-packed road. The sergeant looked at some of the men who were more seriously wounded than he was. He was well enough to sit instead of lying flat on his back on one of the stretchers. His side ached, his head swam a little from the morphine which the medic had given him. He leaned back, smoking a *papyros*. The tobacco tasted bad to him. It was too flat. His mind flashed back to some of the American soldiers he had met in Berlin, toward the end of the long war with the Nazis. He tried to remember the names of their cigarettes—they had tasted good. One had been called "Lucky" he believed. One kind that he remembered—he had liked its taste—had had a picture of a camel on the package. He had taken his grandsons to a zoological park once and shown them a camel, told them how he had smoked cigarettes with the picture of this animal on the packet.

He leaned back and drew the smoke from his *papyros* into his lungs and tried to imagine that it was an American cigarette instead. He looked out and saw the spot of ground where Comrade Private Ivan Meliscovitch had been shot by the Pakistani sniper—two men from the sergeant's own platoon had got the sniper an hour and three dead Russian soldiers later. As the sergeant closed his eyes, trying to forget the bumping of the truck, he wondered if Ivan Meliscovitch had ever smoked an American cigarette . . .

Chapter Ten

"I think it a perfectly charming idea, Mr. Ambassador," Mrs. Justin Colbert-Smythe effused. "Everyone had planned so long and hard for the charity dance—and with the Russians coming now . . . Well, heaven knows what the founding homes here will be forced to cope with."

"I'm so glad you approve, madame," Ambassador Bruckner smiled. "Now, if you ladies"—and he smiled at the tight circle of aging matrons around him—"will allow me, I must confer with some of my associates in the library." He made a slight bow and started to walk away.

"About the world war that's coming—Daddy?"

Bruckner turned, seeing his nineteen-year-old daughter, Cheryl, at the edge of the group of older women, the young French intelligence attaché she had been seeing for the past six months now at her elbow, looking slightly uncomfortable.

"You're being an alarmist darling," Bruckner said, walking toward his daughter. She was the hostess for the evening. "Isn't she?" he said, turning toward her companion. "Isn't she being an alarmist, Charles?"

"As you say, Monsieur Ambassador—isn't she?"

Bruckner glared at the younger man a moment, then leaned toward his daughter and touched his lips to her cheek. He did not like Charles Montand—the young man was not what Bruckner considered a good intelligence man. Talked too much, and then there was always the chance that Montand was seeing his daughter in order to spy on the American Embassy. Montand had started seeing her in earnest just after the embassy in Pakistan had become a listening post for the Soviet occupation on the neighboring Afghanistan border. A great deal of heavy U.S. intelligence was flowing in and out of the embassy. Cheryl, despite her age, and because her father was a widower, Bruckner thought bitterly, was in the same position of many ambassadors' wives—she knew too much.

"I have to go, darling," Bruckner said, his tone brightening. "You see that this last dance here goes well, hmm? Remember, our plane leaves at six A.M."

Then, turning to Montand, "I suppose we won't be seeing you again, Charles—at least not in the immediate future," he added, trying to mute the cheerfulness in his remark.

"Ahh, but you will, Monsieur Ambassador. I am being posted to our embassy in Washington. A promotion."

"Ohh," Bruckner said, forcing a smile.

"*Oui*. I knew that this would be pleasing to you. With your lovely daughter's permission, I can go right on seeing her." Montand lit a cigarette from a small silver case and Bruckner smiled again—he hated men who carried cigarette cases.

"Well," Bruckner said, edging away from his daughter and the French intelligence man, "on such good news, how can the two of you bear standing here talking with an old man like me? You should be out celebrating."

"Celebrating, Daddy?" his daughter whispered, looking down into the champagne glass she held in both hands.

Bruckner looked at the pale blonde hair, the hint of blue eyes under her long lashes, the delicate bones of her face, the tiny but determined chin. It was as if his wife had been reborn in his daughter. Bruckner's wife had died at the moment of Cheryl's birth.

"You're so much like your mother," Bruckner whispered, dismissing the young Frenchman beside his daughter from his mind. "Even to her stubbornness." Bruckner kissed her on the cheek again and walked away.

As he moved along the corridor toward the library, he glanced through one of the picture windows and across the darkened lawns and beyond to the other side of the dark bulk of wrought iron fence separating American embassy territory from Pakistan. There were vans and cars on the other side, and he could see lights for news cameras. The reporters had been there for twelve hours, ever since the United States and several of her allies had announced the intention of leaving the Pakistani capital. Official business was being left in the hands of the redoubtable Swiss. Almost bitterly, Bruckner realized he would be forced to say something to the reporters either when he left in six hours, or else at the airport.

Bruckner stopped at the double doors to the library and pulled down on his waistcoat. He hated formal wear. He placed both hands on the doors and pushed them open with a flourish.

"Gentlemen," he said briskly, then walked across the oriental rug toward his desk, nodding individually to each of the men waiting for him—the French, the British, the West German and the Swiss ambassadors. "I hope you gentlemen like the cognac," he said, whisking the tails out of his way as he sat down in the leather chair behind his desk. "Here, Reinhardt," he started, reaching for the cognac and starting to rise. The Swiss ambassador waved him back down.

"It is my doctor—and my wife. She spies on me for him. No liquor. A horrible way to live," the Swiss ambassador concluded, sucking on a dry pipe, the sound annoyingly loud to Bruckner.

Pouring a few ounces of cognac into a large crystal snifter for himself, Bruckner cleared his throat, then said, "I, ah, I imagine you all know what this is about?" Then turning back to the Swiss ambassador, he added, "I'm sorry we're leaving you with all our troubles, Reinhardt."

"That is part of being Swiss," the man said, gesturing with a casual wave of his right hand. Then he looked back to his pipe.

"I'm sure I speak for all my colleagues when I say that our governments will certainly not forget the kindness, Reinhardt. Then, on to business, hmmm?"

"Arnold?" It was the British ambassador. "What's your American CIA saying? Our chaps assess it as the Russians going full tilt. Will that mean war?"

Bruckner sat back, looked at the Englishman, then the Frenchman beside him, then at the others. "I hope not. But the Russians must be stopped. The president and our State Department are in touch with all the governments involved—the prime minister, the French president, the chancellor—I don't know, in all honesty."

"Will your president commit the American forces, as he has so indicated?" the French ambassador whispered through a cloud of cigarette smoke.

"If the answer won't leave this room," Bruckner began, knowing that it would, "then yes. Some of our rapid deployment forces are already preparing for take-off from Egypt. All they need is the word."

"And vat is this word," the West German said, his hands folded across his massive Bismarck-like stomach.

"There's a time deadline, actually, isn't there, Arnold," the British ambassador interjected.

"Yes—true," Bruckner said, staring into his cognac. "Less than a day, now." He transferred his gaze to his watch.

"Where did it all go wrong, *mes amis*" the Frenchman said, lighting another cigarette on the glowing tip of the nearly burnt out one between his fingers.

"What? Sorry, wasn't listening," Bruckner said, absently.

"I said, where did it go wrong?" The Frenchman stood and walked toward the window of Bruckner's office, parted the heavy drapes there for a moment.

"Where did what go wrong, Serge?" Bruckner asked, his voice suddenly lacking conviction.

"We are all logical men. The Russians are, too. And suddenly the end of humanity is upon us," the Frenchman whispered, his voice even and emotionless.

"I say, Serge—all this poof about the end of humanity—really," the British ambassador droned.

"He is right," the West German said, his voice rough.

Bruckner stood up and walked around to the front of his desk, then sat on its edge. Staring down at the oriental rug, he said slowly, "You realize that it takes hundreds of hours to make a rug like this? The art is almost lost. Like engraving. No one wants to devote the effort to it anymore."

"Then I am not the only realist here," the Frenchman said, and as Bruckner looked up, their eyes met.

"I will take a glass of cognac now," Reinhardt Getsler, the Swiss ambassador said.

"What? Oh, certainly Reinhardt," Bruckner said, reaching for the cognac. When he started to pour it, he noticed that his hand was shaking so badly that the cognac was spilling. The Frenchman walked over from the window and took the snifter and bottle from him.

"Serge," Bruckner said, ignoring the others in the room for a moment.

"*Oui,*" the Frenchman answered, his hand rock steady as he poured the cognac for the Swiss ambassador, then passed the bottle around the room.

"Is your man, Montand—is he only what he claims to be with my daughter? I've got to know."

"Do you mean is he spying on you through her? No. Montand is not."

"Thank God," Bruckner said. "I'd hate it if she'd been cheated. You understand?"

"*Oui.* You can know she has not been cheated of that one thing." Then, putting his hand on Bruckner's shoulder he added. "I have known you since before Cheryl was born. Her mother was not cheated of that one thing either, *mon ami.*"

Bruckner's hand stopped shaking. The cognac in the snifter he held settled into a smooth pool at the bottom. Without looking up, he whispered, "I have a few formal things that the secretary of state wants us to work out—in just a moment though." He emptied the glass.

Chapter Eleven

"All right. Let's just pretend we did a shakedown run and we'll all rest easily. The electric boat fixers here wouldn't let us down," Captain Mitch Wilmer intoned quietly into the microphone. He could hear the faint echo of his own voice coming back to him through the open doorway leading from the bridge over the intercom speaker just beyond. "We're going down now and Mr. Billings, the exec, tells me the water's fine. Anything you need to know, I'll keep you posted. Wilmer out."

Snapping the microphone back into its mounting bracket on the console dominating the central core of the *U.S.S. Benjamin Franklin's* bridge, Wilmer turned to the young man standing just below him by the seated corpsman, saying, "All right, Mr. Billings. You're on. Take her down, Pete."

"Aye, aye, sir," Billings snapped. Then, "Prepare for negative buoyancy. All ahead one-quarter. Check the trim on the starboard diving planes, Smith! Let's get those tanks going. Blow number two and number four. All right, blow one and three. Secure."

A smile crossing his lips, Wilmer cut in on Billings. "I'll be in my cabin for a minute, Pete." Glancing at his Rolex—just about an hour out of New London, Connecticut, now, he saw—he snatched up his baseball cap with the gold braid on the bill and left the bridge. He caught sight of the new sonar man. The man seemed pretty competent. Then he walked down the companionway and to his quarters.

Letting himself in, he snapped on the light, walked past the smaller compartment where he slept and straight toward his desk at the far end of the main cabin. He tossed the baseball cap on the small easy chair, walked around behind the desk and sat down, snatching a thumbnail full of Copenhagen snuff and slipping it into the pouch in his left cheek. He glanced at the photo of his wife and two daughters on his desk.

Fishing in his trouser pocket for his keys, he found the right one and opened the large false drawer at the bottom of the right pedestal of the desk. Bending down to see, he twirled the combination on the small safe there, opened the fireproof door, and reached inside, past his log, for the envelope he'd been given. Wilmer closed the safe, then the desk, and ripped open the manila envelope around the Top-Secret seal. Inside, was a smaller, white envelope. He opened it. On letterhead from the chief of Naval operations was printed a single word: "Morningstar.

"Wonderful," Wilmer muttered to himself. He put the orders down on his blotter and opened the safe again. This time he had to get out of his chair to reach all the way into the back of the safe and work the combination for access to the interior compartment. Tucked inside was a packet of bulging envelopes, each with a code word printed in the upper left-hand corner and stamped again across the closure flap—just as a precaution, he'd been told, that in haste someone didn't open the wrong orders.

"Let's see," he muttered again. "Hippodrome, Indiana, Igloo." Then, flipping through more of the envelopes, he realized that someone was ignoring alphabetical order. "Poker" was in front of "Barricade."

But then he found what he was searching for.

" 'Morningstar,' " he read aloud, then checked that the envelope was perfectly sealed and checked the code name in the upper left-hand corner and across the seal. He stood and walked to his cabin door. He locked it and threw the bolt. Orders were orders, he thought. Going back to his desk, he opened the envelope.

The coordinates in the first paragraph startled him. Using the old Perry route past Baffin Bay and Greenland, he'd intersect the Nautilus polar exploration route—the same route Byrd had used in part—bypassing Franz-Josef Land. Then he'd strike out across the Barents Sea toward the Kanin Peninsula. His target lay 67 degrees north, 31 degrees east, near Murmansk on the Kola Peninsula. The icepack would be above the *Ben Franklin* until she was halfway out of the Barents Sea.

"Wonderful," he said again. There were submarine pens near Murmansk and Archangel and those were his targets.

"Captain . . ." The voice on the intercom was that of Pete Billings, his exec.

"Captain here," he switched. "What is it, Pete?"

"Probably nothing much, sir, but the Russians sure got a whole hell of a lot more trawlers out here than usual."

"Figures, Pete," Captain Wilmer sighed. "Don't get into a fender-bender with the con. I'll be along in a minute or so. Keep me posted if you need to." Wilmer switched off.

"Trawlers," he muttered. Why the Soviet Navy still relied so heavily on trawlers was beyond him. Soviet satellite tracking was just as good as its American counterpart—or was supposed to be—and subs could be tracked by infrared from space a lot more accurately than sonar from the ocean surface. Shrugging his shoulders Wilmer replaced the orders, noted what had transpired—including the trawlers—in his log book, then closed the interior and exterior safe doors and locked the desk.

Putting the keys back in his pocket, Wilmer reached reluctantly into the bottom drawer on the other side of the desk. His 1911A1—slightly oily to the touch—was there, next to its shoulder holster. Standing up, he slipped the harness over his head and left shoulder and settled the strap across his chest, checked the .45 for a full magazine and empty chamber, lowered the hammer, and put the pistol away beside his left armpit. He snapped the strap of the holster closed over it. Wilmer had never liked guns, felt uncomfortable wearing one, and doubted that if he ever needed to use the pistol, he could hit anything with it after all these years.

He reached down to the intercom and flipped the switch to call the sub's hailing system. "Attention, all hands, this is the captain. We are now officially on alert. Section chiefs, report to your stations. All officers, meet with me on the bridge in ten minutes." He started to click off, then thought better of it and added, "We'll be going under the ice on this run, coming up near the Soviet mainland." Technically, he was disobeying the standing orders by telling this to the crew, but made the command decision that everyone would be better off knowing something. "We are not on a war footing. I repeat, not a war footing. So take it easy. Wilmer out."

He snatched his hat as he walked to the door, then passed into the companionway. He passed a seaman first class on his way toward the bridge and noticed that the man was nervously eyeing the .45 automatic he carried. Wilmer smiled at him, murmuring, "Everything's jake."

Wilmer spent a long time on the bridge, then retired again to his cabin, not bothering to eat, telling Billings, "Wake me before we're too close to the ice, Pete." Wilmer tried sleeping, couldn't, then took two sleeping pills. He disliked the way his mouth would taste afterward, but rationalized their use since he would get little rest once under the ice, and after that—he didn't know . . .

There was knocking on his cabin door. Wilmer sat bolt upright, then wiped his hand across his face. Another reason he hated sleeping pills was because they always caused him to dream. And worse still, all he could ever remember of the dreams were that they were horrifying, but he could never remember why.

"Yoh," he shouted, and the knocking stopped.

"Approaching the icepack sir!" The muffled voice on the other side of the door he recognized as that of Dan Kimberly, a chief.

"Gotcha, Dan," Wilmer rasped, his mouth dry. "With ya' in a sec'." Feeling his face again, he decided on a quick shave. He swung his feet off his bunk and into his shoes and went into the bathroom. Five minutes later he was going along the companionway, the .45 back under his arm.

On the bridge, he saw Billings, walked up behind him, and said, "You get any sleep, Pete?"

"No, sir. Figured I would after we got under the ice."

"You're lucky—I can never sleep worth a damn under the ice. I think I'm claustrophobic or getting that way after all these years. Hell of a thing for a submariner, isn't it?"

"Yes, sir," Billings said.

Turning around, Wilmer looked to the man beside the most exotic of the consoles, the ice machine with the long technical name everyone shortened to "Watchyamacallit," the machine that gave a constant readout on the thickness of the ice overhead.

"Got the watchyamacallit all revved up, Henderson?" Wilmer asked.

"Aye, aye, Captain."

"Okay," Wilmer said, then turned to Billings. "Take her under the ice, Pete."

As Wilmer leaned back against the railing on the central island, he told himself again that there was no real change. You were still under tons of water—just tons of ice over that. And surfacing was possible—unless the ice was too thick. And you always rode the instruments like a mother hen looked after her chicks; only, under the ice, the instrument readings had to be more precise and their readings could change more quickly.

An hour later, just as Wilmer was preparing to get Billings to take his promised sleep, the new sonar man called out, "Blip, approximately five hundred off the starboard bowplane."

"Five hundred what, man?" Wilmer rasped. "Sing it out!"

"Make that five hundred—four seventy-five yards now, sir."

Wilmer was already standing behind the sonar man, Billings off to his right behind another console operator.

"Russian, Captain?" Billings asked.

"Hell if it's American—unless we got submarines they haven't told me about. Yeah, Russian, all right. Looks like this is kind of a busy street, huh?" Wilmer turned to Billings, then glanced back at the scope in front of him.

The man working the console tugged at his earphones, saying, "Captain, I'm pickin' up something. I can't be sure what it is."

"Gimme that," Wilmer said, his words harsher than his tone. He took the earphones and twisted them around so he could hear; then looked down at the scope.

"Did a pinch on sonar once, a long time ago," Wilmer recited, slowly.

Turning to Billings, he rasped, "Load up number one and two with conventionals, and ready number three with—" Dropping the earphones, he shouted, "Dammit—that was a torpedo being launched!"

"Captain! We got it on the scope here! Comin' right at—"

"Hard starboard—all ahead three quarters. Make that all ahead full!" Wilmer shouted. The Russian torpedo slicing through the water off the port bow sounded just inches away when it made an echo along the length of the hull. Wilmer, Billings, and every man on the bridge watched along its path as if somehow they could see it.

"Fire one! Fire two!" Wilmer snapped.

Chapter Twelve

"Zero deviant flux on my signal. Ten, nine, eight—"

Mikhail Vorovoi watched the entire firing complex from the steel-railed mezzanine with a sense of satisfaction that was evident in his smile. As the technician droned off the countdown for activation of the laser charge through the particle chamber, Vorovoi could already see in his mind's eye, the Army drone aircraft being set free on auto pilot miles away toward the upper atmosphere, the warheadless missiles being launched from the Ukraine uncounted miles away.

"How do you feel, Mikhail?" a voice said. He turned, saw the hand on his shoulder, looked into the icy blue eyes of the blonde-haired woman beside him, the white lab coat poorly concealing what he had found with her almost every night since they had first met when she'd just come to work on the project. "Your first test on multiple targets, and both missiles and planes. You should be proud, Mikhail Andreyevich, *dushenko*."

"Elizabeta," he whispered, "you know what this means. If my particle beam weapon passes this test, soon it will be operational, and then nuclear war will have become obsolete. Its threat will not hang over us anymore like a plague waiting to break. In just a few years, it will be these weapons that both our country and the Americans will rely upon! No more radiation, no mass murder!"

"You still see this as a road to peace, Mikhail, I know that," Elizabeta whispered.

"Odyin!" The technician shouted the final number. Then: "Switch on, charging, one-quarter, one-half, three-quarter, full power. Boost on number three!"

"Myir," he found himself saying, "Peace. It is at hand, Elizabeta," he murmured, holding her small hands in his. "I must go down on the floor and fire the beam personally—I must."

Their eyes met, and she smiled. He leaned toward her and quickly kissed her cheek, then ran toward the steel ladder that led to the firing arena. He took the ladder rungs two at a time, jumping the last three to the stone floor, then raced toward the center console.

"Here—go, move aside," Vorovoi said to the technician. "I will take charge personally." His dark eyes focused on the instrument panel, the gauges, the indicators, the computer readout diodes. "Boosting ionization twelve points," he shouted, twirling one of the nearer dials. Punching the button for visual via the polar orbit satellite link he anxiously searched the screen, spotting first the low-altitude dot that he knew was the first aircraft, then the second aircraft. Soon— he watched the screen intently—he would see the missiles.

"Capacitance function readout!" he called out.

From behind him, a voice called back, "Ten to the fifteenth capacitance, to the sixteenth, seventeenth—" there was a long pause—"ten to the eighteenth—"

"Hold at that," Vorovoi interrupted.

"Ten to the eighteenth and holding capacitance, zero flux," the voice called back.

His eyes scanning the monitor, Vorovoi saw what his instruments already confirmed—the two unarmed missiles were streaking through the sky toward the drone aircraft. "Designating targets— now! Grid 83, target alpha. Grid 19, target beta. Grid 48—correction, 49—target gamma. Grid 27, target theta— lock!"

He leaned back, waiting, wanting desperately for manual firing mode, but knowing that the true test of his particle beam weapon system and its potential for light-speed pinpoint accuracy lay in the computer firing mechanism as well as the weapon itself. "Automatic target acquisition and destruction on my mark—six, five, four, three, ready, one. Mark!"

He closed his eyes, his hands fanned in front of them a moment. Then, ignoring the dials and gauges and digital computer readouts on the console, he fixed his eyes on the monitor. Target alpha, the nearest of the low-flying bomber aircraft, exploded in a burst of light and vaporized. Almost in the blink of an eye, target beta, the second drone aircraft, vaporized. Vorovoi started to search out the first missile, third target in the firing sequence, but before he could locate it, there was a bright flash. Quickly, he spotted target theta, the last of the four. The angle was right, and he could see the knife edge of the particle beam—it looked like something from an American space movie, he thought. He had seen several American films in Stockholm years earlier when he was there for a scientific conference. " 'Deathray,' " he murmured. The second missile vaporized in a bright flash, the camera whiting out a moment from the light.

There was total silence in the firing control center, except for the incessant whirling and buzzing of the computers and the climate control system which latter was needed for the proper working of the machines. Vorovoi stood up, looked toward the mezzanine, and saw Elizabeta beaming at him. Her smile was something Mikhail could never forget. Locking his fists together over his head, he jumped into the air, screaming, laughing. And, suddenly, the technicians, the military guards—everyone around him—were applauding, shouting, laughing.

"We have entered the new age!" he cried. "Peace!"

Chapter Thirteen

"As you were, gentlemen," Rear Admiral Roger Corbin said absently as he entered the tiny briefing room. The dozen or so naval officers crowded together had started to rise.

"Admiral Corbin!"

Corbin turned around, pushed a bony hand through his graying blond hair, and said, "Yes, Commander," then, squinting to read the name plate, added, "Abramson."

"We've just had confirmation, sir, that—"

"I know, Commander. I'm the one who confirmed it." Then, raising his voice, Corbin started toward the platform at the front of the room, saying, "All right, gentlemen, let's get this thing underway. I'm due at the White House"— and he glanced at his digital watch—"in fifteen minutes."

He lit a cigarette and waited as the room quieted. The gathering of high-ranking Naval intelligence personnel knew him, except for a few faces, like that of Commander Abramson. Corbin began, "The Nuclear Regulatory Commission just confirmed what our own satellite infrareds and other sensing devices already showed. A large-sized nuclear device was exploded just a few miles beyond the estimated perimeter of the polar icecap—just about where the *Benjamin Franklin's* position should have been, according to its last radio beacon relay via satellite. Also, there's a Soviet sub—what the hell's the name of that?" He turned to the lieutenant.

The young man consulted his notes, knit his brow a moment, then looked up. "The *Volga*, sir—it's a *Potemkin* class nuclear sub."

"Right," Corbin continued. "The *Potemkin*—I mean the *Volga*—well, it's off our tracking plots and missing. Could have been a collision, could have been the Russians attacking. There's no way to confirm without pulling another sub off position and going in to take a look-see. Can't do that now. I'll officially label it a nuclear accident, a collision, confer with the Russians, what-have-you. But my personal assessment—and it's just a gut level reaction—is that one of them lost their nerve and opened fire, then the other one returned. I knew Wilmer, commander of the *Franklin*. A little edgy about his job, but a good man. He wouldn't have opened fire first. I bet on the Ruskie commander. Intelligence put him down as a David—pronounce it Dah-*veed*?—Antonyevich Kosnuyevski. Kind of a new man, on his first line command. Could be the sort of thing a guy like that would do. They're on alert status, too."

"Sir," a lieutenant commander from the rear of the room shouted.

"I know your questions before you ask 'em—tell me if I'm wrong." Coughing and stomping out his cigarette, then pausing to light another, Corbin said, "About seventy megatons—means at least one of the reactors went up along with nearly all the warheads on both boats. U.S. Geological Survey, our own people, Oceanographic and Atmospheric Admin people—nobody knows what's going to happen. Should hike the tides, might lose a lot of ice into shipping lanes, could make some minor short-term climatic changes. Not too much crap in the atmosphere as best as we can tell at this time. Answer your question, Commander?" Admiral Corbin smiled, glancing back at the man.

The man only nodded.

Chapter Fourteen

"All right, guys, take off your coats, whatever. The president's on the hot line with the Soviet premier. Told me to get the briefing started."

"Thurston, what the hell I hear about the Navy blowin' up a submarine?"

Thurston Potter glared at Secretary Meeker. What the Commerce Department was doing at the intelligence briefing was beyond him, except for the fact that the president and Commerce Secretary Meeker were lifelong friends.

"Mr. Secretary, I'll come to that." At times like this, Thurston Potter realized, he painfully felt his twenty-eight years. Two Ph. D.s didn't make any difference to the Pentagon people, or to most of the rest of the inner circle of presidential advisors. Potter looked at his watch. In twenty-five minutes he had a press briefing, and by then had to brief all the men assembled in the conference room and get everyone straight on the stories for the media people.

"Maybe I can answer Secretary Meeker's question," Admiral Corbin said from the opposite end of the table, a cigarette waving in his left hand.

"Why don't I?" Potter said. "But, thank you, Admiral." Then, turning toward Meeker and the others, Potter began, "The Navy didn't blow up a submarine, Mr. Secretary, gentlemen. They happened to meet a Soviet submarine. Our *U.S.S. Benjamin Franklin* apparently came in close proximity of the Soviet craft *Volga*. The *Volga* is of their top-of-the-line boats. We don't know for certain whether they collided or fired on one another. I think we should agree officially on a collision story, at least for the press, at least for today. If we say that in light of the current information, we may consider it a collision we'll be safe in case the facts contradict us later. Also, we might be able to use the tragic deaths of several hundred U.S. and Soviet seamen as a tool toward calming things down on the Pakistani question. And we need that. The radiation from the thing—explosion would measure at the same as about a sixty or seventy-megaton bomb. It shouldn't pose much of a health problem. There should be some tidal aberrations—Oceanographic and Atmospheric Admin is drawing up something for the press on that now. But, basically, it looks okay. Any questions so far?"

Potter looked around the room. Several of the men shook their heads. He continued. "Now, to bring you up to date on the Pakistani situation. Our embassy people should be flying out of there just about now—along with French, British, and West German diplomats. Others may be with them. It's a little after six A.M. their time. There's about eighteen hours left on the president's deadline for troop commitment against the Soviets. We're not planning anything terribly major—some rapid deployment strike-force personnel working in conjunction with Pakistani forces. What we are doing is honoring our defense treaty with Pakistan and showing the Russians that we mean business. It would take at least seventy-two hours to position a sizeable force over there. I'm talking about a force that could pose major opposition to the existing Soviet ground forces, and we're on alert for that—Admiral Corbin's people indicate the Soviets aren't building up terribly in the Persian Gulf, but we are. However, not so much as to force them beyond their present strength.

"So what the hell are we doing then?" Meeker said, lighting a cigar and mumbling something that Potter didn't understand.

"Well, Mr. Secretary, the important thing right now isn't so much what we or the Russians are doing—that's pretty much following the patterns both nations expected at this juncture. India's position has become the important variable—and a possibly dangerous one right now. How many of you are familiar with the Indian Ultimatum?" Potter looked for nods or a show of hands. There was some indication that many of the military personnel in the room were at least aware of it.

"Basically," Potter said, "the Indian government sent a communiqué to the U.S., the Soviets, and the Pakistanis. All were identical. If the Russians haven't begun a withdrawal to beyond the Khyber Pass by the deadline that the president set, India will introduce troops into Pakistan to secure Pakistani borders. They believe that the Soviet presence there poses a threat to Indian internal security. Now, we asked the Indians, both formally and informally, to hold off on that. The premier said she wouldn't. The Russians sent a copy of their note to us unofficially. They told her that they had no designs on Indian territory. Unofficially, we told her that we agreed with the Russians, and that in this instance they were telling her the truth. All India did was to respond with a second note—an addendum to their original ultimatum. In essence, it said not to forget India's nuclear capabilities and that were the situation to warrant nuclear intervention, it wouldn't be ruled out."

"Oh shit," Admiral Corbin muttered, but loud enough that Potter heard him at the opposite end of the conference table.

"Yes, Admiral. Oh shit, indeed. And then we got this," and Potter reached into a sheaf of papers and pulled a copy of a telex from the stack, holding it up. "The People's Republic of China—which as you all realize has remained silent throughout this entire unfortunate situation—has informed the Soviet premier that, if need be, China is prepared to side openly with India and support U.S. policy in Pakistan. And, should such become necessary, with military aid. Langley—the CIA people there—they say the Chinese are massing troops on the Soviet border already."

Potter looked around the room, then suddenly felt quite disgusted with the conference and the company. He said, "I think Admiral Corbin put it well a moment ago."

Smiling, Corbin lighted another cigarette.

Chapter Fifteen

"Can't your driver make this thing move any faster?" Rourke said, leaning forward in the seat, the muscles in his face and neck taut, his eyes set.

"You've lived on the Atlantic Seaboard too long, John. You're a southener."

"What, Major?" Rourke interrupted. "Oh, you mean the snow? How it ties things up?" Then, leaning back into the passenger seat beside the RCMP inspector, Rourke sighed, his voice almost a whisper. "Yeah, maybe you're right. How far are we from the airport?"

Rourke leaned forward, rapping on the glass that separated him from the driver. The dark-suited young man slid the panel open with his right hand, without once taking his eyes off the swirling snow and knotted, unmoving traffic along the Toronto airport feeder. "Sir?"

"Masterson, what's your guess on time and distance to the terminal?" Rourke asked in his accustomed soft-spoken manner.

"Time, sir?" the chauffeur asked. "At least an hour and a half. And the terminal is right out there, sir. Less than a mile away."

Rourke snapped his next question. "Masterson, what's that open area like? I mean, would it be heavily drifted? How high if it is?"

"Shouldn't say more than a foot at the greatest, Mr. Rourke. I run out here quite a bit for gentlemen such as yourself. Never took particular notice of the ground, but it should be pretty level—grassy in the summer time."

"Thanks," Rourke muttered, then leaned back again.

"You're not—" the major started.

"Why not?"

"Well—the snow! The cold out there—you want to get to the flight you're scheduled for in one piece, and—"

"I want to get *home*. That's my *big* concern right now and sitting here for another hour or more isn't going to do *that*—it won't get me home," he added. "Now, maybe my *flight* can't get off the *ground* in this *storm*—I don't *know*. But we both listened to that radio. A couple minutes ago we both heard about those two submarines colliding. What if that wasn't a collision?" he asked. "What if the reports were lies? What if those were missile exchanges that caused the explosion under the icepack? What about that ultimatum by India, and that unconfirmed report that China plans to side with us against the Soviets?"

"But, surely—"

Rourke, leaning into the flame of his cigarette lighter and firing up a cigar, squinted into the smoke and looked at the RCMP inspector. "Major, I've got a wife. I've got a son and a daughter. I've got a survival retreat that just might save their lives if we get into a world war. Now, my wife Sarah doesn't know how to find the place. I've checked it all very carefully." Rourke's voice was low, almost menacing. He stared at the major. "If the Russians go after big targets, the section of northeast Georgia where my farm is should be safe from direct hits. Residual fallout should be light there. You can check air flow charts yourself and confirm that. But I'm still gonna have to get them out of there pretty fast, or else it'll all be no good." Rourke pushed the power button on the window and looked outside, then turned back to look at the man beside him. "I'm no good to anyone just sitting here. If I were you," Rourke said, pointing to the red flasher on the dashboard, "I'd have Masterson there flick on that little Mars light you've got, turn this thing around, grab your families, and get the hell out of the urban area. You might be sitting smack-dab in the middle of a ten-mile radius of ground zero right now."

The car had come to a complete stop in the snow and traffic.

Rourke opened the door of the Mercedes sedan and stepped out, shouldering into his down parka. "Trunk unlocked?"

"Corporal Masterson, help Mr. Rourke," the major ordered.

As Rourke started to turn away, the major said, "You really think it's going to happen, John? War, I mean."

Rourke leaned into the car, pulled his right glove off and extended his hand. The major took it. "Yes," Rourke said. "I hope we'll see each other again sometime."

Rourke walked around to the trunk. Already—though no vehicles were moving in the traffic jam and heavy snow—motorists immediately behind them were honking, as if the trunk being opened and a man taking his luggage was somehow adding to the delay.

As Rourke leaned down for his aircraft aluminum gun cases, he heard a man's voice behind him. "Hey—what are you doin', Mac?"

Rourke turned around, looking up. The voice belonged to a man in a worn brown leather jacket. He was burly and bearded. A stocking cap was cocked on the back of his head.

"You talkin' to me?" Rourke asked, quietly.

"You're the only bloody fool standing around out here gettin' your grips from a damned Mercedes—yeah. *I'm* talkin' to *you*."

"Just wanted to be *sure*" Rourke said, his voice low and even as he set down his gun cases.

Rourke's right hand flashed out then, his fist connecting with the side of the bigger man's lantern jaw. The blow was a quick, short jab, and Rourke followed it with a short-arm left into the man's midsection, then a quick right crossing into the jaw.

As the big man started to go down, Rourke caught him under the armpits and eased him into the snow. "Watch your head," he muttered.

Turning back to Masterson, Rourke took his two gun cases, the smaller, attaché-sized one under his left arm, the longer case for the rifles in his left hand. Rourke extended his right hand to Masterson, saying, "Pardon the glove. Good luck, friend."

"And—and to you, sir. You're really going to walk over there, across that?"

"No," Rourke said, the corners of his mouth raising slightly, his lean facing cracking into a smile. "No, I figure that even with the luggage and all, I can still jog it over there—except when the snow gets deep in the drifts. Be seein' ya!"

Rourke boosted his large flight bag into his right hand and threaded his way across the next lane of traffic and onto the shoulder and over to the guard rail. There was—as best as he could make out with the snow cover—a sloping drop of about fifteen feet to the ground level below. He squinted against the glare of headlights and the blowing snow. Across the open space, he could make out the edge of a parking lot. Beyond it was what looked like a hotel, and beyond that, the nearest of the airport terminals. "A little over a mile," he muttered to himself. He lifted his flight bag over the guard rail and let it drop over the side. It slid over the snow. "Not too deep," he muttered again. The long gun case was next. His Colt semi-automatic collapsible stock sporter and the 7.62 mm SSG special rifle, both locked securely in its foam-padded interior.

The long gun case slid down almost like a toboggan, Rourke thought. "Should have ridden it down," he laughed to himself. He stepped over the rail. Losing his footing halfway down the gentle slope, he intentionally let himself fall backward, skidding to the bottom of the slope on his rear end. He stood and dusted the snow from his clothes. Then he looked back up to the level of the highway. He could see Masterson and the RCMP inspector standing at the guard rail.

Rourke made a long, exaggerated wave and, without waiting for them to return it, picked up his rifle case and his flight bag, and started out in a slow jog across the snow.

The snow was drifted heavily near the center of the open expanse as Rourke jogged on. The height of the drifts forced him to slow to a broad stride, a deliberate commando walk. At times, when the drifts were above his knees, he fought the snow, raising his feet high, placing them down slowly to test the footing. His trouser legs were soaked and plastered cold against his skin, but, mercifully no snow had entered his cowboy boots. As he passed the center of the field, the drifts got smaller. As he neared the edge of the snow, he spotted a high fence, snow piled on the other side, apparently from plowing. This separated the parking lot from the open field. It was easy going for him again, and he broke into a jog as he neared the fence.

The snowbank on the opposite side of the fence cushioned the impact for his baggage when he heaved the three cases over. He took a step back and jumped against the fence after he had tossed a snowball against it to be sure it wasn't electrified. Catching the toe of his boot in the chainlinks and holding on with his gloved fingers, Rourke pulled himself up to the top of the barrier and jumped over, coming down in the snow bank. Brushing himself off again, he gathered up his things and started across the parking lot. Climbing the fence had tired him, and now he heard the noise of a vehicle behind him. Turning, Rourke spotted a pickup truck with airport maintenance markings on the door. He stopped as the truck skidded to a halt beside him.

Rourke could see the driver leaning across the front seat and pushing open the passenger side door. "Need a lift? American, ain't you?"

"Yeah, I'm American," Rourke said, nodding. "But, no thanks—good night for a walk—terminal's not too far. Probably faster on foot. Thanks anyway."

"Suit yourself, mate," the driver said, nodding and muttering something Rourke didn't quite catch.

Rourke reached into his pocket, snatched a cigar, and lit it with his Zippo. Looking over the glowing tip and across the lot, he could see the entrance to the hotel-like building he'd spotted from the roadside. "Half a mile," he muttered to himself, picking up his flight bag and walking on.

Chapter Sixteen

"So, we talk again, Mr. President. I, too, prefer the voice link rather than the standard hot line. Now, what troubles you?"

The president of the United States, his coat hung on the back of his chair, his vest unbuttoned, his tie at half-mast, leaned back and put the heels of his shoes on the edge of his desk. He stared at the ceiling of the Oval Office a moment, then began. "Mr. Premier, you are right. We have talked a great deal in these last few hours. I am happy we are of like minds regarding the voice link. When this crisis has passed—as I know that it will," the president said emphatically. Too emphatically, he wondered? "When this has passed," he began again, his tone milder, "I look forward to the voice link as a means of broadening the dialogue between your desk and mine."

"Mr. President?"

"Yes, Mr. Premier?"

"I think you are about to remind me that less than six hours remain before you introduce troops into the Pakistan affair. And you wish to inquire if I personally know about the unfortunate situation between your *Benjamin Franklin* undersea boat and the *Volga*. I do—and I know your deadline, too."

"Sir," the president began. "Ambassador Stromberg and I had a long talk when he was here not long ago. I asked him his personal assessment of you—as a person. You might be surprised to learn how highly he speaks of you."

"You have a good man in Ambassador Stromberg. I would like to hire him from you. But we do not agree politically."

"I don't agree politically with all my ambassadors all the time, either, Mr. Premier. But the point I'm trying to make is that he says you are a man of good will. Well, so am I, sir. I want us to settle this thing here and now if we can. I think we can both agree that we're pushing things a little far this time. Those men aboard your submarine and ours—regardless of how it happened—let's let their deaths become a bond between our peoples. Let's learn from that tragedy to avoid an even greater tragedy. Do you agree, sir, that we should do that?"

The connection was silent a moment. The president could hear the premier—quite a bit older than he—breathing heavily on the line. Then: "In principle, of course, I agree. But coming from principle into fact must be our goal. I would be a madman if I wished to have our two nations linger on the brink of war. But there are other variables—ones which you either wish to ignore or about which you are sincerely less than informed."

"These are, sir?" the president said, swinging his feet from the desk and craning forward in his chair.

"Our particle beam weapon. We have ringed Moscow with these. We have—and this is perhaps something I should maintain as secret information but I choose to reveal it—just completed a test to eradicate the one minor shortcoming of the system. We have tested it against varying altitude high-speed targets in multiple sequence. Four targets, Mr. President. All of them vaporized."

"No disrespect intended, Mr. Premier, but the system would be useless against multiple re-entry vehicles. You must know that. We have our sources."

"We have our sources too, Mr. President. We know what is necessary about your MRVs—we can defeat them. I have, though, no desire to see which of us is correct. You must see that."

The president ripped open his "conscience" pack of Kools from his center desk drawer, lighting the first cigarette he had smoked in three months. He sucked the mentholated smoke deep in his lungs, then spoke again. "I see, sir, that you must realize we are not bluffing. I have already taken steps—which your own intelligence can verify—to interject our tactical response forces at the time the deadline comes about. I have also placed all American forces on alert, prepared for massive intervention in the Pakistan area should Soviet troops not withdraw."

"Then," the Soviet premier said, his voice very tired, "we are like two young fellows trying to prove themselves over a young woman. We will push at each other, brandish our fists, give the angry glances—and see who backs down or fights. The Soviet Union will not back away. I had entertained the hope that your ambassador could convince you of the sincere motivations for our move into Pakistan. Apparently, you chose to ignore this. My hands are tied. I will not be the first to start a war, if that gives you any comfort, nor will I immediately react with Soviet nuclear forces if your American troops do indeed move into Pakistan. But if Soviet lives are threatened, then I must take whatever action conscience dictates as necessary. Please call me again if there is some new development—I shall do the same. The interview is almost over, I think?"

"Yes," the president sighed. "Yes, I'll keep in contact with you, sir."

"But one thing more, Mr. President."

"Yes, Mr. Premier?"

"I wish to make a demonstration. We are using, if I understand correctly, the primary satellite for our talk. The others are still operative?"

"Yes—but I fail to see what you're driving at, sir."

"The voice you will hear on the line is a technician—he cannot hear our conversation though we can hear him. Do not be alarmed. This is a mere test."

The president sat bolt upright as he heard a heavily accented voice—young sounding, either a woman or a boy, droning, "Ten, nine, eight, seven, six, five, four—"

"Mr. Premier! What is going on? I demand—"

"Zero. Mark!"

The president sat back in his chair, the communication link dead, a loud buzzing sound having started before the connection automatically cut out. He hung up the phone. In a moment, his intercom buzzed. "Sir?" It was one of the secretaries.

"Yes, what is it?"

"I have the premier on the line again."

Clicking the intercom off, the president snatched up the red phone. "Yes?"

"The particle beam weapon. We will reimburse your country for the satellite if you feel that it will prohibit any tension resulting from this demonstration. But, please, check with your communications and electronics intelligence personnel. The satellite was vaporized by a high-frequency particle beam."

"That proves noth—"

"That is sad," the premier remarked. "I had hoped that it would." And the line went dead, the premier's phone clicking in the president's ear.

"Marian!" the president rasped into his intercom.

"Yes, Mr. President?"

"Get Mr. Antonais, my science advisor."

"Sir, he's already on line six."

"Put him on," the president said, lighting another cigarette.

"Mr. President?" the Greek-accented voice said.

"Dmitri—did they really—?"

"Yes, Mr. President. The Con-Vers One was vaporized at precisely—"

"Never mind that," the president said. "Get over here. I'll need you."

The president hung up the phone, leaned into his intercom, and said, "Hold all calls for about two minutes. I've got to think."

He switched off, stood, and walked toward the window, looking out into the rose garden. At this time of year, he thought, it wasn't terribly pretty.

Chapter Seventeen

"Some sort of policeman, are you?"

"What?" Rourke said, turning away from the window and his view of the snow-littered runway and looking at the blond, ruddy-cheeked man beside him.

"I asked if you were some sort of policeman?"

"No," Rourke said, starting to turn away.

"Saw you back in the terminal—so covered with snow, looked almost like you'd walked," the man began, laughing.

"I did walk—what's so funny?" Rourke said.

"Well—I meant with the aluminum cases and all. I'm a shooter myself, you know. Gun cases, weren't they?"

"So what?" Rourke said. Then noticing the belligerence in his own voice, he forced a smile then as he did.

"Well, not the ordinary person can take guns in and out of Canada. Rifles, yes, but not handguns. That was what you had in that smaller case, wasn't it?"

"I was up here doing some teaching with the Mounties," Rourke explained. "Brought the guns along for a short thing with one of their special units." He did not mention the counter-terrorist squad.

"Going to Atlanta on business. How about you?" the man said, changing the subject.

"I have a place down there, and a farm in the northeast part of the state. So I'm going home."

"Oh. Well, I won't be home for two weeks. Things to do, a living to make, all that."

"It sounds fascinating," Rourke said, turning away to glance back out onto the runway. He turned back and stared toward the front of the first-class cabin, hearing the speakers coming to life. "This is the captain speaking. Ladies and gentlemen, I'm sorry for all the delays caused by the snow, but it looks like we'll finally be getting off the ground in just another few minutes. I've just been in radio contact with the tower, and we're cleared for approach onto runway four. Looks from here like there are about four planes ahead of us, so it shouldn't be long before we get final clearance for that long-awaited take-off. Weather reports just south of here show gradual clearing, and once we're over the Great Lakes area, then heading down toward the Smokey Mountains, the weather moderates quite a bit. Atlanta's Hartsfield Airport, our destination, shows clear conditions, present temperatures of high forties with a morning low of the low forties and clear and warming for tomorrow. Since we will be getting underway, if you may have loosened or undone your seat belts, we ask that at this time you check that they are secure. And that all trays and seats are in the upright position. I'll leave the no-smoking signs off for now, but please observe them once we actually get underway. Should you have any questions now or later, please check with the stewardesses as they pass by. Management tells me because of the delays here, cocktails will be complimentary for this trip once we're airborne. So please enjoy your flight and thanks for traveling with us."

Rourke stared back out the window, automatically tugging at his seatbelt. He realized almost bitterly that if the war came, his lifelong battle of nerves with his wife would be ended. His position would be vindicated. A smile crossed his lips as he remembered something someone had said about the bitter taste of victory—he would have rather lived a lifetime in peace, his time and money invested in survival equipment, and the retreat itself having been all part of being foolishly over-prepared.

"You know, I've spent a long time analyzing world affairs," Rourke said.

The ruddy-cheeked businessman beside him turned and looked at him, saying, "What? I'm sorry?"

"I said I've spent a long time analyzing world events. I prepared for this—read everything I could get my hands on, trained—"

"What?"

"I knew this was coming." Finally, then, as if for the first time he noticed the man beside him listening to him, Rourke turned and said, "Have you been listening to the news? The radio?"

"What? All the war talk? Just sabre rattling, my friend. I wouldn't worry over it. Not a bit."

"Oh, you wouldn't, huh? Well, I was just going to suggest that maybe you get off this damned airplane and go home and take care of your family—just in case it isn't all talk."

"You really did walk through the snow just to get aboard. My God, fellow, you take this Russian stuff dreadfully seriously, don't you?"

"Yeah," Rourke said, terminating the conversation and turning back toward the window. "I guess I do."

*****

"There's another communiqué from the Indian government, Mr. President. Just came in over the telex."

"Read it to me, Thurston," the president said, sitting down at his desk.

Potter whispered, "All right, sir, It says—'"

"Just the essentials," the president said.

"Yes, sir. They say that at the expiration of your deadline, they'll utilize a low-yield nuclear device— tactically. It's mostly as a symbolic statement of their entrance into the conflict with the Soviets and their intention to resist their incursion into Pakistan at all costs."

"That's crazy. Get me the Indian ambassador right away."

As Potter left, the president turned to his national security advisor, Bernard Thorpe. "Bernie, what do you think?"

As Thorpe started to speak, Commerce Secretary Meeker cut in. "You'd better get out of here up to somewhere we can count on your bein' alive long enough to direct the war effort, Mr. President."

Bernard Thorpe, wire-rimmed glasses in his hands, his pipe out but still clenched hard in his teeth, said, "Much as I hate to agree with Mr. Meeker, Mr. President, he's making good sense. If India uses a nuclear device, maybe we can still avoid a war. Pakistan, though, might be tempted then—I understand they have them ready. No really effective delivery system, though. But that could start it. What if another pair of submarines collides or attacks each other? What does Mr. Antonais say about the Soviet particle beam systems?"

"Dmitri says they could be operational, but that the destruction of the communications satellite was just a planned shot—could have been working it out for hours in advance and probably were. Won't be any match for our MRVs. But I don't want to get that far. I don't think the premier wants that, either."

"Are we going to back down then?" Thorpe said.

"I'm going to call the premier again. Maybe we can work out a compromise. Bernie, tell Marian to have my special plane called up just in case I want to get over to the mountain."

Meeker, standing up, exhaling hard and tugging at his tight necktie, said, "Good move, Mr. President. If those suckers want to play poker, well then, let's play."

*****

The Soviet premier sat at his desk. The lights of his office were out except for the small desk lamp and its circle of yellowish light. "You are sure of this?" he asked.

"Our intelligence realized the importance of this, Comrade Premier. It has been investigated and investigated again. There can be no doubt," the woman said.

"You have been a major with Intelligence for long, Gospozha?"

"Yes, Comrade Premier," she answered uncomfortably.

"How nice for you." Then, looking back at the deciphered message in his bony hands, he said, "So the Pakistan Army has a nuclear device and will destroy a dam lying in the path of our forces. Has anyone bothered yet to inform the Pakistan Army that this will force the possibility of total war?"

"No," the woman said, thoughtfully. "No, Comrade Premier. Or, at least, I have not been so informed."

"Well, well . . ." The premier blew smoke into the circle of light. "The American president just tried calling me, but I was unavailable. He left word he would try again from his hardened mountain retreat—his bomb shelter. I suppose that I, too, should go to my bomb shelter. He can reach me there. You

71

are a credit to your sex, Comrade Major. Please advise my staff that I instructed you to avail yourself of some refreshment on your way out."

The premier picked up the phone on his desk, dialed, and spoke into the receiver. "Alert the helicopter pilot that I shall be needing his services shortly, and make all other arrangements. I wish the emergency meeting of the Politburo advisors, my science advisors, and other members of my senior staff to begin in five minutes."

He hung up the phone and blew more smoke into the patch of light on his blotter.

Chapter Eighteen

"Major, excuse me."

Major Nikita Mikhailevitch Porembski turned and stared at the young female lieutenant. "Yes, what is it?" he asked.

"My good friend, Comrade Major. He is with the troops at the Pakistan front. I was wondering . . .?" The blonde-haired girl left her question unfinished.

The man squinted as he looked down into her blue eyes. "I can tell you nothing. I know nothing. There is an alert order. The rumor is that we may launch against the American mainland and selected American allied targets. I do not know anything beyond that. The rumor is only that, Lieutenant. It is your lover for whom you worry?"

The girl looked away, her eyes cast down. The major touched her shoulder lightly. "There is a special meeting underway in the Kremlin, I have heard. Perhaps, some decision will come of that. Perhaps not. Are you on duty?"

"No, Comrade Major. I went off duty an hour ago, then came here."

"To Army Headquarters?" The major's voice was filled with incredulity. Then, "You must love the young man a great deal. He is an officer?"

"Yes, Comrade Major," she said, her voice low. "We attended school together."

"Come—I have not eaten. The canteen has food. I too am off duty now. We can talk, Lieutenant. Will you come?"

The young woman looked up into the major's gray eyes. "Yes, Comrade Major."

The two officers started walking back down the hallway, in the direction from which the senior officer had just come. "You remind me of my niece," the major began.

Suddenly, there was shouting from the end of the hall. A young lieutenant was running toward them, his hair flying in his wild eyes. "There is war! There is war!"

As the young man passed them, the major put his arm around the young woman beside him. He watched her eyes stare blankly down the corridor after the rapidly disappearing young man.

"War," he said quietly, and the girl looked at him.

*****

Aboard his helicopter, flying through the night, the Soviet premier shone a small pen light onto the sheet of yellow paper he held in his left hand. He preferred the flashlight to the overhead dome light. On the yellow paper, not bothering to abide with the lines there, he had written several items, all of which he had discussed with his Politburo advisors, his science team, the military staff—all in a very brief time before he had boarded the helicopter.

Item one had been the particle beam weapon. He did not trust it; neither did the military. Only the fanatic young scientist was convinced—and had pleaded—that it would mean an end to nuclear war. The premier had decided he could not trust the weapon to bring down the American ICBMs, especially those with multiple reentry vehicles— multiple warheads. He would gamble on launching Soviet missiles if the Indians or Pakistanis struck with nuclear weapons first.

Item two had been the Chinese. This had forced the nuclear option, and had amended item one. He had felt compelled to attack the United States first, for the Chinese would surely attack if the Indians or Pakistanis used a nuclear device, and intelligence indicated that the Pakistanis were ready to do so within the hour to stop the Soviet advance. The sad thing, the premier thought, was that he had already ordered the advance stopped. His troops had secured the territory they had originally intended to take, and there was no need for further advance.

Item three. He turned off the pocket flashlight. He could see the words even in the total darkness. The first missile would launch in approximately fifteen minutes, just as he reached his shelter.

"How many dead?" he muttered—in English so the pilot would not understand.

*****

"The following special broadcast is a tape of a message prerecorded in the Oval Office just minutes ago. The president of the United States."

Sarah Rourke walked past the television set and sat down. Michael and Ann were asking questions. "Hey, Mom, why is he on? It's supposed to be—"

"Shh—let me hear this," she said, holding up her hand to silence the boy.

"I want to sit on your lap," Ann, said.

"Fine," Sarah whispered, as if by talking aloud she would lose her grasp of the moment.

"Good evening, my fellow Americans," the familiar voice began. Silently, Sarah Rourke looked at the president's face and thought how old he had gotten in the years since he had assumed the office. She had met him once and remembered him as looking twenty years younger.

"If you are now hearing this message, it is because something of vital concern to the American people has just taken place. We are all aware of the heightening world tensions in these past few days and weeks—these past few hours. It would appear now that the possibility exists of Soviet military action to some degree or another against the United States. If you are now hearing this message, it simply means that we have elected to take the precautionary action of placing you, the American people, on alert to this possibility. It does not mean that war has been declared, or that attack is imminent. It does mean that it would be prudent to tune to your local Civil Defense—"

Sarah Rourke stood up, slipping Ann from her lap.

"Mommy!"

"Quiet—please," she said, going to the stereo and punching the AM button and turning the dial to 640. The president's voice was coming through on the radio as well. "—their directions. The American people have endured many hardships over the past in the defense of liberty, and their response has been one in which future generations of Americans have always taken great pride. Let whatever events transpire be so recorded as well. And let us pray that these few simple precautions will be required for only a brief period. By keeping tuned to either 640 or 1240, by following the simple advice broadcast by Civil Defense, we shall all endure the events which are taking shape in as peaceful and secure a manner as conditions allow. I am ordering, for the protection of all Americans, that martial law be in effect in areas of high population density; that all sales of liquor, firearms, ammunition, explosives, and other controlled substances—with the exception of medication—be curtailed. To heighten the effectiveness of Civil Defense measures—"

Sarah Rourke put her hands over her ears. She wanted to scream. Tears welled in her eyes. She looked at Michael and Ann—Michael looked so much like John. Ann was crying, Michael looked afraid.

"Come here, children," she said. She looked at the digital clock on top of the TV set, hearing the president's voice again, telling her not to be afraid. She stared at the clock. "Maybe Daddy's plane has landed already," she whispered.

Michael, his voice low for a boy his age, said, "Don't cry, Mommy," then put his arms around her neck. She leaned her head against her son's chest and cried anyway.

Chapter Nineteen

"This is the captain speaking, ladies and gentlemen. I—ah—I don't quite know how to say this, but according to Atlanta tower, for reasons of national security, our flight and other flights stacked currently at the field are being diverted inland. I'll ask that you check your seat belts once again. We'll be moving out of our holding pattern here and taking a new flight plan. Our projected landing is in Phoenix, Arizona. I want to apologize, on behalf of the airline, for any inconvenience this may cause you, but also assure you that transportation back into the Atlanta area as soon as such can be arranged will be taken care of, as will accommodations for you in the Phoenix area. The reason behind this rerouting, as best as we can determine, is a currently unsubstantiated report that the Soviet Union and the United States, fifteen minutes ago, officially broke off diplomatic relations."

"What the hell is going on?" Rourke said, his voice low. His right hand stretched across the florid-faced businessman beside him and held onto the arm of a stewardess.

"Sir, I really can't add anymore to what the captain has said." Her well practiced airline hostess smile had vanished. He looked at her, released her arm, and turned back toward the window.

The captain's voice came on the speaker again. "Ladies and gentlemen, this is Captain Stewart again. I'm picking up something cutting across our frequency with Atlanta tower. It indicates that Civil Defense is alerting the Atlanta area that approximately fifteen minutes ago satellites indicated a massive Soviet Intercontinental Ballistic Missile launch against the U.S. mainland and Western Europe."

The intercom system was still on—Rourke could hear it humming. But beyond that and the engine vibration noise as the aircraft climbed into the higher, thinner air—the lights of Atlanta vanishing in the distance below—all was silent.

Then he heard a scream. The woman sitting across the aisle screamed again, grasping at her throat with both hands. Rourke ripped open his seat belt, pushed rudely past the man in the seat beside him.

Other passengers started screaming. In the aisle now, Rourke shouted, "Quiet down! This woman is having a heart attack—what's your excuse?"

He bent over her and loosened the tight pearl choker at her throat. The old woman was starting to gag. Forcing her mouth open, Rourke reached two fingers inside and got her tongue back up out of her throat. A stewardess was at his elbow. "Are you a doctor?" she said.

"I trained as one. See if there's another doctor aboard. Hurry!"

As Rourke started to bend toward the old woman to give her resuscitation, he stopped. The fluttering of the pulse at her neck had stopped. She was no longer breathing, and her eyes were fixed and staring. Leaning over her Rourke hammered his fists down over her chest. He could hear the stewardess's voice behind him, "What are you doing?"

Without looking at her, Rourke rasped, "I'm trying to get her heart started again."

He kept at it for several seconds—and nothing happened. "Stewardess!" he shouted.

"Yes, sir. There wasn't another doctor aboard. Can I help?"

Rourke glanced at the young woman over his shoulder. "Yeah. Find me a hair dryer and something to plug it into—hurry."

"A hair dryer?"

"Yeah," he rasped. "A hair dryer, electric razor—something like that."

In a moment, the stewardess was back beside him, a gun-shaped hair dryer in her hands.

Snatching the appliance, Rourke ripped out the cord, then using a small pocket knife, split the cord and stripped away the insulation, exposing an inch of wire. "Plug this in when I tell you to—but don't touch these ends or let them drag against anything."

Putting both hands on the neck of the older woman's dress, he ripped the garment down the front. "Okay—plug it in," he said. Then, turning to the stewardess, he took the electrical cord and gingerly touched both exposed ends together until they sparked.

"Now," he whispered, "don't let anybody touch her." He touched both ends to the woman's chest. Her body bounced half off the seat. Leaning forward, he listened for her heart. Taking the electrical cord again, he touched the ends once more to the woman's still chest. Her body lurched up, then back down into the seat.

"She's breathing!" the stewardess cried.

Rourke wrapped the electrical cord around his fingers and yanked it from the socket. "Try to make her comfortable," he said, leaning down and listening to the woman's heart, then holding her wrist for the pulse. "Keep her mouth clear. Have one of the passengers watch her to make sure her chest is rising and falling. And you better go tell the captain to set us down as soon as he can. This lady here needs a hospital."

"I can give her oxygen."

"Save that for when she needs it—she's breathing okay for the moment," Rourke said.

He pushed his way through the passengers who had crowded around them and walked toward the center cabin bathroom and let himself inside. He stared at his face in the mirror a moment, catching himself against the small sink there for support as the plane suddenly lurched downward.

The president and Thurston Potter raced across the White House lawn toward the special short takeoff and landing plane which the president had ridden only once before during a Civil Defense exercise. It was called the "Doomsday Plane," and aside from the president and his advisor there was room for only the pilot and a co-pilot and one more passenger—the Air Force sergeant who accompanied the president everywhere he went. A small black rectangular case was in the sergeant's hand, and, as always, handcuffed to his wrist. Inside the case was a small radio telephone unit; its battery was charged once a day and the leads checked at least that often. Using the communications device, the president could give the coded verbal attack order for a massive nuclear launch.

The president—his advisors had told him the Soviets had undertaken their own massive launch— had not used the box yet.

79

When they were all aboard the Doomsday Plane, Potter shouted, "Are you going to use the box, Mr. President?"

The president strapped himself in. The Air Force sergeant was beside him. The plane had already started to lift off. The president shouted over the engine noise, "Not yet! There's still a chance. Not yet."

As the plane angled upward and cleared the White House grounds and the tops of the buildings, there was a sudden shudder and the plane raced forward. "We'll be at the mountain in less than ten minutes," the president shouted. "I've got a call going out to the Soviet premier."

"But, sir, none of us *wants* this. But some of their submarine based missiles could be re-entering the atmosphere by now," Potter pleaded.

The president held up his right hand for silence. Above the engine noise he heard a low whistling sound. The engine noise of the aircraft suddenly intensified. "We're speeding up," the president said, half to himself.

The whistling sound, despite the engine noise, grew louder. The pilot's voice was coming over the speaker from the radio set on the fuselage beside the president. The president, the Air Force sergeant, and Thurston Potter stared at it. "This is Major Hornsbey, Mr. President. My radar just picked up a missile—a big one, it looks like—coming out of the east on a trajectory with the center of Washington."

The president tapped the Air Force sergeant beside him on the shoulder. "Harry, give me the box now."

Afterward, as the president handed the communicator back to the sergeant, who replaced it in the box, he said, "Gentlemen, I think it would be proper for us all to take a moment for silent prayer." Only the drone of the engine filled the small cabin for several moments. Then, the sergeant and Potter looked over at the president. Potter opened his mouth to say something, but stopped. The president was saying, in a barely audible whisper, "The Lord is my shepherd, I shall not want . . ."

*****

80

Sarah Rourke, Michael, and Ann, carried bottles of water down into the cellar. Ann was crying. She didn't like the cellar. Sarah sat down in the corner on the floor between two inside walls, Michael on one side, Ann on the other. The transistor radio, tuned to the Civil Defense station, was on the floor under her raised knees. She leaned forward and pulled the hide-a-bed mattress that Michael had dragged down the stairs for her closer to them.

"Now," she said quietly, the voice of the Civil Defense announcer droning on from the radio. "I'm not going to say this is a game, children. This is very serious. We're going to pull the blanket up over our heads, then the mattress. That's in case some damage should be done to the house. But we're almost seventy miles from Atlanta, and I don't think the damage will go this far. Now, remember, keep under the blanket and the mattress. There might be a very bright light that could burn us, but it will go away after a few seconds. That's what the radio announcer said. There might be a very strong wind—that's why we're down here in the cellar just in case some of the windows get blown in. And there may be a really loud noise, so when I put my arms around you, I want each of you to put your hands over your ears and keep your mouths open. Okay?"

"We'll be all right, Mama," Michael said, putting his arm around her neck. "I'll take care of you and Annie."

"I know you will, Michael," she whispered. "Now—give me a hand with the blanket and the mattress."

With Michael's help, Sarah pulled the blanket up over their heads, then awkwardly reached around and hauled the mattress over them. She turned on the flashlight and let it rest between her legs beside the radio. Sarah's left arm was around Ann, and she drew Michael toward her, then put her right arm around him. She circled them with her arms and put her hands over her own ears. All of them had their heads down. She could hear that the radio was still playing, but she could not make out what the announcer was saying.

Very suddenly, she felt the ground underneath them tremble. She held the children more tightly, looking into the dim light cast by her flashlight to make sure their ears were protected. She had to force Annie's hands up over her ears.

There was a rumbling, and even with her hands over her ears it seemed to grow steadily louder. She drew the children's heads down into her lap and bent her body over them. Michael began to squirm.

The sound grew louder, the trembling beneath them intensified and suddenly she felt warm— warmer than she should have felt under just the blanket and the mattress. After what seemed like a long time—though her watch showed that it had only been a minute or less—the noise started to die down and the trembling subsided.

She waited, realizing she'd been holding her breath. "Children, I think it's passed."

As she started to sit up, there was a whooshing noise and the sound of smashing glass from the house above them. She'd been on the fringe of a hurricane once, she recalled. And the sound she heard now was like that—a strong wind. The house began to shake, the sound of glass breaking from upstairs in the house grew louder. She could feel things falling on her back as she bent her body over the children. Ann was crying, and Michael was asking questions. Sarah Rourke wanted to scream, but she didn't. "It will be all right," she whispered. "Daddy will be here soon." But in her mind, she realized that if her husband had been anywhere outside and unprotected, he was probably dead. Her heart forced her to dismiss the idea as soon as it came to her. Until she knew otherwise, she told herself, she would believe her husband was coming for them—however long it took him.

Sarah Rourke whispered to the children, "Daddy will come."

Chapter Twenty

"My wife? The children?"

"They are fine, Mr. President. We'll be perfectly safe here," Thurston Potter said, walking over to the president and sitting down on the easy chair opposite the couch where the president sat.

"Is everyone here at Mt. Lincoln?"

"Your chief of Staff, Paul Dorian is here, sir. Mr. Thorpe is here. Lieutenant Brightston is playing with your youngest son, running movies for him. Rear Admiral Corbin and his intelligence people made it."

"What about Secretary Meeker?" the president said.

"As best as we can determine, he was going to get his wife—we don't think he made it. Washington is all but gone. The vice-president, Mr. Sneed, didn't make it either, sir. They couldn't get him out of the hospital at Bethesda in time. The operation he was having was at the critical stage."

"My God, Meeker, Sneed! How many millions, Potter? Any estimate yet?"

Before Potter could answer, there was a knock at the door.

"Yes—come in," the president said, his voice high-pitched.

Rear Admiral Corbin stepped through the doorway. "Mr. President, I've got a preliminary situation report."

"What about casualties?" the president said, lighting a cigarette.

"Well, too early to tell, Mr. President. It looks like they made a massive launch, but with the exception of a few strategically important cities, primary concentration was on our military targets—not on population centers. Some reports from the Midwest indicate that neutron devices might have been used— so the real estate up that way should at least be somewhat salvageable."

"What sort of damage are we inflicting on them?"

"Major cities, major industrial complexes—but they got way too much of our stuff while it was on the ground. I think we lost this one, sir," Corbin concluded.

"*This* one?" the president said, and he realized he was smiling absurdly. Then, quietly, he said, "Admiral Corbin, don't you realize there isn't going to be another one?"

*****

Rourke shouted, "Everyone, look away from the windows and put your heads down—protect your faces, your eyes!" Staring out the window as the 747 had crossed beyond the Mississippi, Rourke had caught a glimpse of something in the air—pale white and crashing downward. As the 747 started rocking and bouncing, Rourke knew his guess hadn't been wrong—it had been a missile with a nuclear warhead. What had been, seconds earlier, the city of St. Louis, Missouri was now gone.

After a few minutes, the turbulence eased, and Rourke looked up. The moans and cries he'd heard were quieting now as he looked around the first-class cabin. People in the window seats—at least a dozen that Rourke was able to count quickly—had their hands pressed to their faces and were screaming or sobbing.

Rourke looked into the aisle as the stewardess who had helped him with the older women earlier came down the aisle. Her hands reached out to the seats to steady herself against the jet's motion. Her face was white, her eyes wide. Rourke reached out and took her hand, leaning across the man next to him as he did. "What is it? You just came from the captain."

"Nothing, Mr. Rourke. Nothing to worry—"

Rourke stood up, stepping past his seatmate and into the aisle. Reaching into his wallet, he fished out one of his identity cards and handed it to her. "You know what this is?"

"It says Central Intelligence—"

"Yeah," Rourke whispered. "Now, unless your passenger list shows somebody else, I'm the closest thing to a government official you've got on this plane. Now, what's up? Pilot and co-pilot were blinded, weren't they?"

"How did you—"

Rourke cut her off. "Only makes sense. They couldn't have looked away from the St. Louis blast in time, too much glass up there anyway. Did the cabin keep its integrity—none of the glass was broken or anything?"

"Yes, but you're right. Neither of them can see. It's on auto pilot now, but with this turbulence—" "Exactly," Rourke said. He made a quick decision to calm the passengers before he checked on the pilots. "Give me the microphone for the speaker system," he said.

He followed her up the aisle toward the front of the cabin, and she handed him the microphone. He pushed the switch and began to speak. "Ladies and gentlemen, my name is Rourke. I am a special employee of the government." Mutterings and exclamations mixed with the cries and sobs. Everyone began shouting out questions at once. He looked toward the window nearest him. "Now, I want everybody to be quiet a minute and listen. First, haul down the curtains on the windows, and don't look outside. Second, if you've got someone seated near you who appears to be having trouble with his eyes right now," he lied, "that should be just temporary. After I'm through talking, get a pillow from the compartment above your seat and try to make the person comfortable. I'm also a qualified physician, so I will be coming around to check on you all. Take a blanket from the compartment and try to keep the injured person warm. Soon, we will come to you and make available whatever medical assistance is required." He paused a moment, then added, "It looks like the United States is under a nuclear attack—"

Another burst of cries. Someone started to scream. Rourke shouted over the microphone. "Now, let's be quiet and let's keep calm! I wish I could say something encouraging about what's going on below us on the ground, but I can't. But for now, we are all reasonably safe," he lied again. "Now—I'd like anyone with flight training of any sort to report to the front of the forward cabin as soon as I'm through talking. Don't panic. The captain has the plane under control, but because of the turbulence from the heat on the ground, he can use some extra help on some of the instruments. Also, anyone with any sort of first-aid training or nursing experience, report up here, as well, as soon as I'm through. We'll need your help to get everyone comfortable and start tending to their medical needs. The stewardesses will come around now with complimentary drinks. I suggest you have one. It's going to be a long night." Rourke handed the microphone to the stewardess.

Several passengers started filtering up toward the front of the first-class cabin. When no more seemed to be coming, Rourke addressed them all, saying, "Okay, let's crowd into the galley. Talk things over. You too," he said to the stewardess.

Rourke walked into the galley and leaned against the counter top, waiting until everyone was inside. When they had gathered, he told the stewardess, "Close the curtains and keep 'em closed," then turned to the six men and women. "Now, does anyone here have any kind of flight training?"

A woman of about thirty raised her hand.

"What kind of training?" Rourke asked.

"I started private pilot training three weeks ago—I've had four lessons in the air. That's all."

"Well," Rourke said, smiling, "that's better than nothing, isn't it?" He bit on his lower lip, searched his jacket for a cigar, found one, and lit it with his Zippo. "Anybody else?"

There were no responses. Rourke said, slowly, "Then I assume the rest of you have had some medical training. Now, the stewardess here will coordinate with you on anything you need that we can get hold of to help. Anybody a nurse?"

There were no responses. "All right," Rourke said, "the stewardess is going to get on the PA system and see who among the passengers has aspirin or any other kind of pain killers. Lay off the aspirin unless nothing else is available. We might find that some of these people have radiation sickness, and the last thing they need is something else to irritate their stomachs. Flush the burned areas on their faces and eyes, use cold compresses, try to make everyone comfortable. Do what you can. I'm a doctor, so if you need any advice, have the stewardess check with me. Now, I don't have a bag or any instruments or drugs or anything, but I can help.'?

Turning to the woman who'd said she'd taken flying lessons, Rourke said, "What's your name, Miss?"

"It's Mrs.—Mandy Richards."

"Well, Mrs. Richards, you and I are going to go forward and see about help-ing the captain and the co-pilot. Okay?"

"I don't know how much help I can be, Mr. Rourke."

"Call me John. Simpler. We'll help however we can."

The stewardess was already starting back down the aisle with large contain-ers of water and towels. The five who'd claimed some medical experience followed her.

Rourke knocked on the door of the pilot's cabin and tried the handle, then walked through, saying to the woman beside him, "Forgive me for going ahead of you, Mrs. Richards."

Rourke stopped inside the doorway. Both the captain and co-pilot were still strapped into their seats. Both men were writhing, holding their faces. The co-pilot was moaning.

"Shut the door, Mrs. Richards," Rourke said softly.

Leaning down, he walked forward and looked at the captain. The woman behind him said, "My God, both of these men are blinded like—"

"That's why we're here, Mrs. Richards. But if we tell all the passengers, they might panic, and that wouldn't do anyone any good, right?"

"Who—who are you?" It was the captain, his voice strained and hoarse.

Rourke leaned down beside the man. "My name is John Rourke, Captain. I'm one of the passengers. The stewardess told me you might need some help."

"You're the doc, aren't you?"

"Yeah, well in a manner of speaking," Rourke said. "But I'm here to help you. I've tested out on military jet fighters, flown a helicopter. There's a woman here with me—Mrs. Richards—who's had flying experience, too. Thought maybe we could give you a hand. If you can stay conscious, maybe you can tell us what to do to keep this thing airborne and help us land it when it's time."

"That's impossible, Doc. The controls on these babies are just too much un-less you know them—I can't talk you through it."

"Well," Rourke said softly, "you'd better hope we can figure this out. By the looks of that fuel gauge, I don't figure we've got more than a couple of hours flying time before we hit empty. And auto pilot isn't going to do much next time we hit a shock wave from a missile going off under us."

"What's the use? We're all dead anyway," the captain said.

"Maybe, maybe not. I don't know. But we can't just commit suicide up here, can we?"

Rourke watched the captain. The man's eyes were closed tight. His face was beet-red like someone with a bad sunburn. "It's no good," the captain said, "but go ahead and try if you want."

"I will," Rourke said, then started unbuckling the pilot and getting him down on the floor at the back of the cabin as comfortably as possible. "Get some pillows, blankets, water, and towels, Mrs. Richards," Rourke said. As the woman left, Rourke moved forward and helped the co-pilot—unconscious now—into a reclining position near the doors.

In a moment, the woman was back and Rourke said, "Work on the captain first. The co-pilot's pretty far gone."

Rourke sat in the pilot's seat and started studying the controls. He hit the switch for the intercom and spoke into the microphone. "This is John Rourke. Could the stewardess, Miss—" and he remembered he'd never asked her name— "the stewardess who helped me a few moments ago report to the cockpit for a moment?"

Rourke looked at the controls, the myriad dials and gauges. He began to believe that the captain had been right. He entertained little hope of getting the plane down. Shrugging his shoulders as he heard the knock on the door, he knew that little hope of success would not keep him from trying. At the back of his mind, as he called out, "Come in," he wondered if Sarah and Michael and Ann were still alive. He chewed down on his cigar.

"What is it, Mr. Rourke?" the stewardess asked.

"Are there any manuals," he began, "instruction booklets—anything that can help me with this thing?"

"The pilots have manuals," she began, then leaned over and reached into a drawer under the instrument panel, "but they're designed as troubleshooting references. I don't know if they'd be of any help."

Rourke glanced at the thick, vinyl-bound manuals the stewardess gave him and weighed them in his hands. "Just the thing," he said quietly, "for trouble-shooting."

Chapter Twenty One

Slowly, Sarah Rourke pushed away the blanket and mattress covering herself and the children. She smelled something—smoke? But no, she thought. It was plaster dust. "All right, children," she said. "I think we can see what's going on now."

Chunks of debris fell from the mattress as she pushed herself up onto her knees. Standing, surveying the littered cellar, she picked up her small transistor radio and shook it—nothing but static. She switched bands. There was nothing on FM. She turned the dial from side to side—still, only static.

"What's wrong with the radio, Mama?" Michael asked. His question was something she could have done without at the moment.

"Oh, I think the ground shaking must have loosened a wire inside it. You know," she continued lying, "these radios are made up of thousands of wires. Your father can tell you about it better than I can."

"Where is Daddy, Mommy," Ann asked, her voice little as the three Rourkes stood there in the partially collapsed cellar.

"Oh, he's coming, honey," Sarah Rourke reassured her.

"It'll be all right," Michael said, putting his arm around his sister.

"Michael," Sarah began, "you stay here with Ann for a minute. I'm going upstairs to look around."

"Can we come? We don't want to stay here."

She looked at Michael, nodded. "All right, but stay behind me. Just in case anything is wrong upstairs." The flashlight—one of John's Safariland Kel-Lites—was still working as if nothing had happened. For a moment, as she focused the beam toward the stairs, the thought amused her. She could imagine her husband, in one of his magazine articles or books, saying, "This Kel-Lite flashlight survived World War III and kept right on working." The thought almost started her crying. She sniffed and started toward the staircase, then stopped. She smelled gas.

"Michael, go back and very gently pick up the water jugs. Hurry, but be careful."

"But can't we get the water later, Mom?"

"No, son, I don't know if we'll come back down here again. I smell gas, and we might be risking a fire. Don't touch anything metal, don't scrape against anything at all if you can help it. Then come back and hold your sister's hand."

Michael returned in a moment and handed Sarah two of the three water jugs he'd brought, then took his sister's hand. "Now, Michael, don't let go of her—no matter what you do. Do you understand?"

"Yes," he started, "but why—"

"Never mind," Sarah said. She looked at Annie, who looked as though she would burst into tears at any minute.

Sarah stooped down to her. The little girl—her hair different from Sarah's, John's or Michael's, a dark honey blond—raised her arms into the air. "Will you pick me up, Mommy?"

"I can't now, Annie. But I will later."

"I want somebody to carry me."

"You're going to have to walk, Annie," Sarah said firmly, then turned back toward the stairs.

Plaster in large chunks and small pieces of wood littered the stairs. She started to push them aside, but thought better of it; they could be nails or some small metal among the debris which could make a spark. Slowly, she picked her way up the stairs.

"Michael!" she screamed, turning and glaring at the boy.

"What did I do?"

"Don't kick that stuff off the stairs. It could make a spark. Just take my word for it and don't. Now, come on—hold Annie's hand."

Annie dutifully grasped her brother's larger hand and walked beside him. As Sarah looked at the little girl's face, she could still see that the girl was on the verge of tears.

Sarah stopped at the closed basement door. The gas smelled stronger. She reached down to the doorknob, then stopped. "What if it makes a spark?" she asked herself, half aloud.

"What is it, Mama," Michael said. Then, "Here —I can open the door for you."

Suddenly, Michael was standing beside her, his hands already on the door-knob, pushing the door open.

"Michael!" Sarah screamed, grabbing the boy and his sister and drawing them against her. The door, the hinges creaking and sounding as though they needed oil, swung open. Nothing happened.

Cautiously, the boy and girl beside her, Sarah stepped into the house. The smell of gas was completely gone. As she looked up and down the hallway, she could see that, apparently, every window in the house had smashed inward. The rooms were littered with glass from broken dishes and vases, the overhead lights—everything was destroyed.

"What happened?" Michael said.

"Some very bad men dropped some big bombs on our country, Michael," Sarah said. "You've heard about the atomic bomb, the hydrogen bomb. Well, they have a lot more explosive force than ordinary bombs. All this mess is from bombs they dropped on Atlanta—and you know it takes us an hour and a half to drive there. So Atlanta was pretty far away." She shuddered as she heard herself use the past tense—"was." The zoo, the museums, the shops and restaurants—a flood of memories rushed over her. The people? Her throat started tightening, and, bending down to the children, she said, "I want us to get a few things and get out of the house. We'll stay in the barn tonight."

"Why would we stay in the barn, Mom?"

"Yeah," Annie echoed, "why are we going to stay in the barn, Mommy? I don't like the barn very much."

"Well," she said patiently, "the gas that we all smelled down in the cellar. Gas could still build up and explode. We'll be safer in the barn. Now, come and help me." Automatically, she started toward the kitchen, but changed her mind. "We're going upstairs to get a few clothes and things just in case we don't get back to the house for a while. Michael, take some jeans, underpants, a couple of shirts, all your socks and two extra pairs of shoes and put them in your back pack. Then get Annie started. Take your sweaters, too."

"It's not very cold out, Mom," Michael started.

She leaned down to the boy and put both hands on his shoulders. "Michael—you're very smart and sometimes you're very grown up. But sometimes I need you to do what I say—exactly what I say. Now hurry and do it. And don't forget to start getting Annie packed too."

She went up the stairs ahead of the children and glanced in their rooms to make sure everything was safe. Like the downstairs, the upstairs looked, she thought, as though a hurricane had struck.

Shouting, "Watch out for broken glass—Annie, stay with Michael," she walked to the end of the hall and the bedroom she shared with her husband—when he was home. She went into his dresser and found the only other gun besides the shotgun that he had forced her to keep in the house. She looked at it, reading the words on the side of it, "Colt's Government Model Mk IV/Series '70," then underneath that, "Caliber .45 ACP." As she held the gun, she wished she'd listened to her husband more attentively when he'd told her about it. She remembered his leaving it there several months earlier.

"Now, this is a Government Model .45," he'd said. "Just a pretty ordinary gun but a damned good one."

"You mean a .45 like the little guns you carry?"

"Yeah," Rourke had said. "Just bigger. Now I know you have trouble with slides on automatics, but I've left one round loaded in the chamber. After you shoot the gun—cock it first—leave the hammer up and just put up the safety. See?"

Sarah had gotten the discussion over with as quickly as possible. Now, she turned the gun over in her hand. It had rubber grips, black, with medallions of tiny horses on them. Shrugging her shoulders, she stuck the gun in the waistband of her blue jeans, shivering a little because the metal was cold against her skin. In the same drawer, she found two extra clips, which, her husband had always told her, were magazines. She took those and a box of ammunition and stuffed them into a large canvas purse, then went into her own dresser and got underwear, some T-shirts, and two sweaters. From her closet, she took two pairs of jeans, identical to the ones she wore. She put two pairs of track shoes into the huge canvas bag as well, then went back to her husband's dresser and took as many pairs of his white sweat socks as she could fit into the case. She snatched up their wedding picture, too, stripped it from the frame, and folded it in fourths, then put it into an inside pocket of the bag.

As she passed the bathroom, she took a canvas bag from under the sink—an old U.S. mail bag—and began stuffing it with soap, tampons, toothpaste, bandaids, and disinfectant spray.

Michael was ready and waiting in the hallway and she checked his pack, sending him back for his sweaters and telling him to grab as many rolls of toilet paper as he could and stuff them in his pack.

As fast as she could, she helped Annie pack, stuffing extra clothes for both children in Annie's back pack. She walked the children downstairs, the water jugs still down at the foot of the stairs where she'd left them, and carried everything into the kitchen. Her husband had insisted on her keeping a supply of freeze-dried foods from Mountain House and similar items, these all in a large duffle bag in the pantry. She grabbed this up, opened the bag, and stuffed a few cans of soup and beans and a can opener inside it as well. "Now," she said, "I want both of you to drink as much as you can of the milk in the refrigerator. I have to get everyone's vitamins and some blankets."

She left the children and ran back into the hallway and up the stairs, getting vitamins from the bathroom vanity and blankets from the spare bedroom. She wished now she'd let her husband buy them the sleeping bags he'd wanted to.

As she reached the bottom of the stairs, she stopped and caught her breath.

"Come on, children," she shouted, then started back toward the kitchen for them.

"I'll put the milk in the refrigerator," Michael said.

"You don't have to darling," Sarah began. "There isn't any electricity."

With Michael carrying more than she'd thought he could, and Ann dragging Sarah's big canvas purse, Sarah started everyone from the kitchen, then thought of one other thing. She reached into the top drawer beside the sink and took the very sharp, Henkels boning knife, wrapped it in a kitchen towel, and slipped it into the duffle bag. She could barely move the bag.

As they reached the end of the hallway, she stopped and turned into the living room, "wait a minute."

She went over to the mantle, grabbed the pictures of the children, and stripped them from their frames. Then she took the double-barreled shotgun from over the hearth and grabbed the box of shotgun shells from the drawer in the small end table.

"Okay," she said, trying to make her voice sound cheerful. "This is going to be quite an adventure." As they stepped onto the front porch, coats on, arms loaded with belongings, she could hear the horses in the barn, whinnying, frightened. And she realized why. In the darkness—although the late- night sky in the direction of Atlanta was bright like a sunset—she could hear the wild dog packs howling. The sound frightened her, too. "Come on, children—let's get to the barn," she whispered.

Chapter Twenty Two

"I have those figures now, Mr. President," Thurston Potter began.

"How accurate are they?" the president asked, sitting back down in the couch.

"Computer estimates based on intelligence data—close."

"All right," the president said, his voice low, "tell me."

Potter began. "Less than twenty percent of continental land-based missiles were able to get airborne. Of the ground bombers, approximately eighty-five percent made it out. Our nuclear submarine fleet and bombers holding at the Fail-Safe point came out okay in terms of doing their job. I have a ratio of ninety-percent effectiveness for the submarine fleet. The bombers got to target, but, apparently, that Soviet particle beam system knocked most of them out."

"I want to know about casualties—us and them," the president interrupted.

"We estimate sixty percent of the U.S. population dead or dying—about 145 million people—"

"Oh, sweet Jesus."

Potter went on, sifting through the papers in his hands, "By morning there should be at least seventy-five times more third-degree burn patients than all pre-war burn centers and fully equipped hospitals could handle. The anticipated deaths as a consequence make up part of that 145 million casualty figure. Add another twenty percent for residual deaths from radiation poisoning. So we get slightly less than 175 million dead within the next few weeks, and that should be the maximum figure. I can go into greater depth, Mr. President. We have a preliminary statistical breakdown."

The president glanced up at Potter, staring into his eyes. "Later Thurston. How did the Russians do?"

"We knocked out sixty percent of their heavy industry, approximately forty percent of their population. And they've still got the Chinese to contend with. Other global casualty figures aren't too complete, yet, but much of the British Isles have been destroyed, some major cities in Canada. Most of France is intact. Nothing nuclear except for a lot of tactical stuff used in West Germany, and Soviet divisions are swamping Europe. But that won't last. The Chinese are really giving the Russians hell on the Sino-Soviet border."

"How about our forces?" the president asked.

"That's not so good, Mr. President. Our European land forces have been pretty much wiped out. But a lot of small units are still fighting independently, and the Pentagon people indicate they'll go on doing that until you tell them otherwise. Most military bases in the continental United States were knocked out, since they were A-Class targets because of their missiles. The really bad news is an unconfirmed report that when the missiles struck on the West Coast, they ruptured the San Andreas fault line and caused massive earthquakes and tidal waves. We've confirmed that New York City was swamped by an Atlantic tidal wave. Estimated casualty figures don't include the San Andreas quakes, but do include the New York disaster."

"Are the Russians coming?" the president asked, his voice emotionless.

"As best as we can tell, they'll make landings in certain safe cities where they used neutron bombs. About twenty-four hours. It's more symbolic than military. They can hold those areas, but just frankly don't have the manpower to do anything else with the Chinese on their rear ends. And they won't have sufficient heavy industry for years to get up enough muscle to actually occupy our entire country. We've got some small independent military units that are ready to go and make the Soviet occupation here miserable. Should be able to keep up fighting almost indefinitely."

"I suppose I should be thankful," the president muttered. "The whole planet could have been blown out of its orbit and plunged into the sun—like some of the scientists have been warning."

"Well, sir, no one got to use all their stuff. The Russians have pretty much stopped targeting us now. May have been a slight axis shift, could result in some radical climatic changes. Can't tell yet. Pretty scary business. Mind if I sit down, Mr. President?"

"Oh, I'm sorry Thurston," the president said, looking at the young man. "Yeah, go ahead and sit."

"Mr. President, what are you going to do?"

The president smiled, saying, "I was afraid somebody was going to ask me that. Well, I have no precedent to guide me. The country, more or less, has ceased to exist as a country. I don't know. What about fallout—any guesses there?"

"Well, sir, we had a lot of scenarios worked out for war, and this comes closest to scenario," and Potter studied his notes. "Eighteen-A. I doubt you'd remember it by that number, but, basically, it looks as though the fallout should stay in bands across the country, and when it settles to the ground, stay that way. Some areas will become nuclear deserts and are estimated to remain that way for perhaps hundreds of years—depending on the exact nature of the warheads the Soviets dropped. Some few areas will have very little danger from fallout. But then of course, almost the whole Mississippi basin was destroyed with direct hits, so the entire midsection of the country is going to be a vast no-man's land for a century or more."

"The planet isn't dead, though," the president said.

"Not as far as we can tell. I don't know if I should tell you what Rear Admiral Corbin said."

"Tell me," the president asked.

"Well—he called it instant urban renewal. Said someday future generations may actually thank us for this. Only the really fit will survive, the weaker types will be naturally cropped out. The land will eventually restore itself."

"He's full of crap," the president said quietly.

*****

The Soviet premier signed the necessary papers for the token airborne invasion of several neutron-bombed cities. Most important would be Chicago, or what was left of Chicago after the seiche in Lake Michigan had produced a tidal wave effect and destroyed much of the city proper. Chicago was the largest of the cities they would occupy; Atlanta, St. Louis, Washington, and other eastern cities had been destroyed by conventional nuclear weapons and would be uninhabitable for—he checked the figures on the radioactive half-life of the nuclear material—204 years. Los Angeles and other western cities were not to be considered. Los Angeles, San Francisco, and most of central California had fallen into the Pacific when the San Andreas fault line had slipped. This distressed the premier. Tidal wave effects had swamped a portion of western Canada; parts of Alaska and were expected to slide toward the coastal areas of Siberia and, eventually, Japan.

The Premier turned off the desk lamp. Unlike the one in his Kremlin office, the light was strong, and it hurt his eyes. Sitting in the darkness, secure in his bomb shelter, he recalled the preliminary casualty estimates for the Soviet Union—some forty percent of the overall population. He closed his eyes—120 million men and women and children had died. And there was still the war with China. In the darkness, where no one could see him, he brushed tears from his great dark eyes.

Chapter Twenty Three

Rourke stood up and turned toward Mrs. Richards who was kneeling on the cockpit floor beside the captain. "You were right." Mrs. Richards looked at him. Rourke went on. "The captain is dead." He glanced across to the other side of the narrow cockpit—the co-pilot had died twenty minutes earlier. "Looks like it's up to us now," Rourke said quietly.

Mandy Richards bit her lip and nodded.

Rourke patted her on the shoulder. "From what I've been able to tell, we've got about two hours of flying time left—less, since we'll need some fuel to get her down, and we'll have to get down to a lower altitude before we can do that."

Suddenly, Rourke held his fingers to his lips, signaling silence. The speaker for the radio was the focus of his attention. He heard a voice coming from it. Ever since he had gone forward to the cockpit and begun trying to decipher the controls, the radio—on every band he'd tried—had been nothing but static. Ionization, he'd believed was the cause. But now there was a voice.

"Excuse me, Mrs. Richards," Rourke said, moving forward and dropping into the captain's chair, then putting the headset on and working the radio controls. "This is Canamerican 747 Flight 601—reading you with some heavy static. Do you read me? Over."

He waited a moment, then the static broke and the voice came back. "This is Buck Anderson—ham operator out of Tombstone, Arizona, Captain. Over."

Rourke smiled. "I'm no captain kid—just a fella" flyin' the plane. Captain and co-pilot bought it with flash burns. Is it possible for you to relay our signal and get us some professional help—maybe from Tucson?"

"There *is* no Tucson," the voice came back. Then there was a long pause.

"Buck," Rourke said, "you still reading me? Over."

"I'm still reading you. But there is no—no Tucson. Everything to the west has either gone into the sea like California did or been flooded. We're on an island out here now."

"Yeah," Rourke cut in, "yeah, I knew your area—was there for Helldorado Days."

"But the water," the boy's voice went on, "it may be rising—not sure if it's stopped. Everyone is dead—I'm sick—the bombs that hit Tucson and Phoenix just wiped them out. As far down as Bensen."

There was a little restaurant in Benson that Rourke had liked. It had made the best pizza he'd found in Arizona. "What's your source for the West Coast thing?" Rourke asked. "Over."

"Ham operator—a girl I knew. We were on when the bombs started falling and she kept on. Somehow I was still getting her. Then she started describing it—horrible."

"Tell me," Rourke said, his voice low. "Over."

"Oh, Mother of God—the buildings started shaking, the ground—from where she was she could see the ground starting to open, and then she went off. After that, I picked up another commercial flight. Told me they were watching from the air—huge cracks in the ground—lava coming up, and then suddenly it all slipped away and there was a giant wall of water. I lost the transmission after that. The pilot said the turbulence was getting bad and cut off, kind of funny."

"Any word on Flagstaff, Buck?" Rourke asked. "Over."

"No—nothing since a Civil Defense broadcast over an hour ago—the whole area around Flagstaff and the Grand Canyon had an eight or nine-point earthquake, and there were bombs still falling."

Rourke just shook his head. "Kid," he said, "you gonna make it?"

"I don't think so—I'm starting to throw up blood—vision is already blurry. I think its radiation sickness."

"It is, Buck," Rourke said.

"That's what I thought."

"I'm sorry," Rourke said.

"I wish I could help you get your plane down. But I can't. Maybe you're better off just crashing—it's hell down here. The air is bad, the water's rising now—I can tell, and—" The voice cut off.

"Buck?" Rourke said.

The boy's voice cut back in. "My generator handle pulled out—sorry."

"Anything on New Mexico? Over."

"Can't make out—" Then there was static.

"Did he die?" It was Mrs. Richards, sitting now in the co-pilot's chair beside Rourke.

"No, Mrs. Richards—we just got into different air space and out of his frequency. No, he didn't die—yet."

"Maybe the boy was right," Mrs. Richards said.

Rourke looked at the woman. "Now, as long as we're alive," he said, "we've got a chance. Once we give up and lie down, that's it."

"My husband was in California," Mrs. Richards said.

"I have a wife and two children back in Georgia," Rourke replied.

"But they could still be alive. I know my husband is dead. Maybe that boy was just a liar," she started. "A liar—he was just lying because he didn't know—it couldn't have just fallen into—"

"I don't think he was lying, Mrs. Richards," Rourke said, quietly.

"Do you think my husband could have survived?" she asked softly.

"Honest?" Rourke queried.

"Yes," she said.

"No—I don't. Even if he was on the right side of the fault line, the tidal wave would have gotten him. I had, I guess, a friend in San Diego—told me once that if the San Andreas fault ever went, he'd be okay. His office and his house were on the continental side. I didn't have the heart to remind him about the tidal wave. See, when those mountains slipped off and all the land on the other side, the impact and the added mass, as well as the slipping motion itself—all that figured in to create a tsunami and then flood the lowland. I don't know where the new coastline will wind up."

"Why should *I* live?" she moaned. "There's nothing left. Nothing to live for. Why live now?" She said it like a chant.

Rourke looked at Mrs. Richards, then slowly said, "That's a question you're going to have to answer for yourself, ma'am. And I hope you can. Now, lets try to fly this plane, and get everyone down, huh?"

He kept watching her. She did not seem hysterical or beside herself, but her eyes filled with tears. Finally, she turned to him, whispering, "Maybe you just said it—we got all those people back there, haven't we?"

"Yes—we have," Rourke said slowly. "And all they've got right now is us."

"What will it be like—on the ground? If we make it, I mean?"

"Well, your guess is as good as mine. But I don't see humanity coming to a screeching halt, if that's what you mean. Maybe civilization, but humanity will find a way of going on. It always has, always will. Now," he said, turning and facing the control panel, "like the man said, let's see if this mother'll fly. You got charge of the instruction book."

Rourke put his hands on the controls, killed the auto pilot switch, and throttled back to get the feel. Suddenly, the plane shuddered.

"Mr. Rourke!" Mrs. Richards shouted.

"That wasn't me, lady. That was the explosion down there." Already, he was hauling back on the controls and throttling forward. "Hit that seat-belt sign, Mrs. Richards, and get on the PA and tell everyone to settle in. I gotta climb before that blast cooks us!"

Mrs. Richards picked up the microphone for the PA, then asked, "Was that another missile that hit?"

"No—we were over an oil refinery, is my guess. It just blew." Almost as the words left his mouth, the plane shuddered, and he locked his fists tighter on the controls. "Hit that seat-belt sign, huh!"

Chapter Twenty Four

Sarah Rourke crouched by the inside of the barn door, her right hand clutching the shotgun, her left arm around both children.

"Who is it, Mama?" Michael whispered.

"Shh," she rasped, looking into the yard between the barn and the house.

Four men and a woman were the object of her gaze. All were in their middle or late twenties, it looked. They stood around a late-model van with a smashed right front fender. They had guns in their hands. She recognized one them—a military-type weapon, an M-16, she thought. It looked similar to a gun her husband used a lot, but the rear portion of the stock was different.

"Hello in the house!" the woman in the yard shouted.

Annie started to speak, "Mommy—she said hello to our house," then started to laugh. As Sarah turned and put her hand over the little girl's mouth, she realized that the five in the yard had probably already heard Annie.

When she looked back into the yard, two of the men were gone, and the other two men and the woman were staring toward the barn.

"Hey—who's in the barn?"

Sarah was paralyzed. If she shouted back, they'd realize—no matter what she told them—that there was no man. But if she said nothing?

"I said, who's in the barn?" The voice was rough and angry.

"I am," Sarah shouted back.

It was one of the men who spoke. "Just who are you?"

"I'm a woman with a gun, mister. Come any closer and you'll find out who I am." Sarah Rourke was surprised that the words had come from her mouth.

Suddenly, from behind her in the back of the barn she heard a voice. "Drop the shotgun, lady—or I kill the kids."

Sarah Rourke wheeled around on her knees, releasing the children and bringing her left hand onto the shotgun. Michael was starting to get up. "Stay still, Michael," she screamed. The man who had spoken—there was another man behind him—was standing in the loft of the barn, the military rifle in his hands.

"Drop it, lady. We ain't gonna hurt ya. Unless you put up a fight."

"You leave my mother alone!" Michael shouted, his voice sounding younger and smaller to Sarah than she'd thought it could.

Behind her, Sarah heard footsteps. Then the woman's voice. "We got you covered, lady—drop the shotgun and move away from it."

Bitterly, with a feeling of great failure, she dropped the shotgun.

"Okay." It was the man who'd talked before from the loft. "Move away from the kids."

"No," Sarah shouted.

"Move—or they get it."

Sarah looked up at him. "No, please don't." Suddenly, she was angry. She knew that John would not want her to beg these people. And she knew that she wouldn't. As she started to edge across the barn floor, she saw Michael out of the corner of her eye. He was starting to walk toward their bags in the corner. No one was watching him.

"All right, lady—on the ground," the man in the loft commanded.

"What you gonna do, Eddie?" It was the woman.

"I'm gonna get me a piece. Then I'll see."

"Not in front of her kids, Eddie!"

"Why, maybe they'll enjoy it." Then—Sarah watched his eyes across the distance that separated them—"Okay, lady—down." Sarah started to drop to her knees, watching the man coming down the ladder from the loft. She had lost sight of Michael, but saw a pitchfork in the opposite corner of the barn, perhaps ten feet away.

"All right, Eddie—me and Pete and Al can go check the house." Sarah watched as the woman and the other two men left. Then she turned her eyes back to the man, who had reached the foot of the ladder and was turned to face her.

"I ain't had no head for a while. Maybe we'll get started with that. Stay right there on your knees, lady, or the kids get it." The man started toward her. Her eyes were looking past him—to the pitchfork. As she turned to look up into his eyes, he shouted "Goddamnit—" and started to fall forward against her. His body fell onto her and she pushed against him.

She saw the boning knife she'd taken from the house—it was buried up to the handle in the man's right kidney. In the same instant, she saw Michael, standing where the man had been a second earlier.

"Take daddy's gun, Mommy!" he shouted. She found herself reaching for it. The dead man was *still* half on top of her, and her legs were pinned. The .45 was in her hands now. She looked to the loft. The second man was already halfway down the ladder. She held the gun, cocked the hammer back, and pulled the trigger. Nothing happened. She held the gun more tightly, pointed it, and tried the trigger again—the gun jumped in her hand. The shot rang in her ears, and the man fell from the ladder, his rifle sailing out of his hands.

Sarah worked her legs under the weight of the dead man and pulled free. She stared at Michael. She knew in the back of her mind that the other two men and the woman would be coming any minute.

"Michael?" She looked again at the knife in the first man's kidney.

"Daddy said that when he's gone, I'm the man of the family."

Sarah Rourke swept her six-year-old son into her arms, holding him tight against her.

"Mommy!" It was Annie screaming. Sarah, on her knees, turned, the .45 Colt automatic still in her right hand. It was the woman. She was aiming a revolver at Annie.

Sarah pulled the trigger on her .45.

The woman screamed, fell back, and the revolver dropped to the ground. Both hands clasped her chest.

"Annie!" Sarah screamed. Then, "Michael! get your sister to the back of the barn. The other two men will be coming."

Sarah Rourke started toward the open barn doors. One of the men was already running across the yard. She fired the .45 once, then again, and the man turned and ran back toward the house.

"It's the broad and the kids!" he shouted.

Sarah fired again, kicking up dust near his heels, but missing the man. She stayed by the barn doors, waiting.

"Give up, lady. We ain't gonna hurt you. Give up or we'll burn down the barn with you and the kids in it!" a voice shouted from the house.

"Mommy?"

"It's all right Michael," Sarah said, surprised that her voice was so even and calm.

She looked down at the gun in her hand, remembering what John had said about the safety catch, and raised it. She saw now why it hadn't fired the first time—John had told her about the grip safety. She hadn't been holding the gun tightly enough. She looked around on the floor of the barn, then walked over to the first man—the one Michael had killed. The thought of that was still hard for her to accept. How one night can change your life she thought. She was proud of Michael for defending her.

She reached down and tried to pick up the dead-man's military rifle. The sling for the rifle was still over his shoulder, and she had to lift his dead arm to pry the gun loose. She read the legend on the left side of the gun. "Colt AR-15." It was like her husband's gun. It was better than the shotgun. She moved what she thought was the safety but the clip started to come out. She pushed the magazine back in and searched again for the safety. She found it and pointed the gun in the direction of the floor and pulled the trigger. The dirt and boards started to fly up and she took her finger off the trigger. "A machine gun?" she muttered. She remembered, then, having read an article dealing with how some people took sporting rifles and changed them to sub-machine guns, illegally. She guessed that this was one of them. Her husband's gun—the stock was definitely different—fired only one shot at a time. She moved the safety lever, then touched the trigger to see if she had it right. The gun fired, but only one shot. She tried the safety lever again. She pressed the trigger and nothing happened. She moved it all the way back, and the gun fired like a submachine gun again. In the second position, it fired one round at a time. She took a deep breath and searched the dead man's clothes, finding four extra magazines. She would have to empty one and count how many rounds they held, she told herself. "But first things first."

Already, she knew what she would do about the two men in the house. There had been others who had drifted by during the night. Outlaws, brigands—just people who wanted to steal. She'd frightened one group away with the shotgun, not even firing it. And she realized these men who had almost killed the children and herself wouldn't be the last. She would have to leave the farm. The pickup truck or the station wagon would only run out of gas. She looked at the two horses, standing peacefully in their stalls—her mind flashed back to the last time she and John had gone riding. She could load the belongings and both children on the horses, and still ride herself.

She turned toward the house and began to walk toward the barn doors. She had to get rid of the men in the house before she could do anything else. Several times through the night, when the wind had shifted, she had smelled the gas from the house. The basement had only one window—a small one that somehow hadn't blown out. The basement still had to be full of gas.

She got down on her knees and put the rifle to her shoulder, setting the selector lever to single-shot. Semi-automatic. She remembered the term. John used it frequently in his weapons articles. She found the sights and lined them up, then aimed toward the house.

The bullet hit the dirt in the front of the house. She raised the barrel, aimed again, and tried to squeeze the trigger—the few times John had forced her to try shooting, he had always said, "*Squeeze* the trigger—don't snap it back."

She squeezed the trigger. She saw a piece of one of the house boards fly off. One of her hanging planters was still attached to the top of the front porch, and she aimed at it. When she fired, the planter moved. She fired again and the planter disintegrated.

"Dammit, lady, keep up that shootin' and we'll burn down the fuckin' barn with you and the kids in it—so help me!"

A smile lifted the corners of her mouth. She would have never thought of what she was going to do if they hadn't threatened—twice now—to burn down the barn. She was going to bum down the house—blow it up, with the men inside.

She pointed the rifle's muzzle toward the small, unbroken window of the cellar, lined up the sights, and squeezed the trigger. The window smashed. Nothing happened. She fired again, then fell back on her haunches. There was a loud roar, then fire belched, first from the small window, then from the first floor of the house. Then a fireball engulfed the house for an instant. Flames leapt skyward. She could hear screams from the house, one of the men yelling, "Gas—I'm on fire!"

One of the men—she thought it was the one the dead woman had called Pete—ran from the front door, his clothes burning. She fired, and he fell over. "I'm a killer," she whispered.

Chapter Twenty Five

"Mr. President," Thurston Potter said. "Mr. President?"

The president of the United States rolled over and opened his eyes. "Thurston?"

"Yes, sir. You fell asleep on the couch."

"Oh—yes. I guess I did. And it isn't a dream, then, is it?"

"No, sir. I wish—"

"What's the current situation?"

"We've just received word, Mr. President. The Russians are broadcasting on a low-frequency FM band that's getting past all the static. We must formally surrender or they'll destroy the few remaining cities. I don't know what to—"

"Well, what is it, Thurston?" The president swung his feet off the couch.

"I don't know, sir."

"If I surrender, then most of the resistance to them will stop—it won't even begin when they land here."

"Yes, Mr. President."

"If I just let them take us, then they can put any words in my mouth that they want, can't they?"

"Well, I suppose so, sir."

"The vice-president, the speaker of the house, all of my cabinet—dead. Dead?"

Thurston Potter squirmed on his heels. "Yes. Yes, sir."

"If I were dead, there would be no United States government to surrender. No one who had the power to surrender. Correct?"

"Well, sir, there were a few members of Congress who were out of Washington. A few may have survived."

"But it would take the Russians forever to find them—if they were still alive. Right?"

"Yes, Mr. President."

"Do we have a way of getting news out?"

Potter thought for a moment. "We could send out some of the intelligence people to spread the word, I suppose. It would be slow, but once it got started, if the news were important enough, the people would hear it."

"That's what I thought. Get me Paul Dorian. Then, after he leaves, I want to see my wife and the children. After that, the chief of the Secret Service detail here. Hurry. You come back with Paul."

The president leaned over the coffee table and took up one of his cigarettes. He was smiling as he lit it.

*****

"All right," Mrs. Richards. I've decided to try to bring this thing down just south of Albuquerque. There's a lot of flatland south of there, and a drop in the desert looks like the best chance we have. I'm betting the Albuquerque airport is finished."

"You can't be sure," the woman said.

"I can overfly it," Rourke said. "You're right." Looking away from the instruments a moment, Rourke said, "Mrs. Richards, take the controls. Don't move anything." He consulted the plastic-covered maps and checked them against his approximate position. "Albuquerque should be ten minutes ahead." Already, as Rourke looked through the windshield and down toward the ground, the sun was starting to rise. The ground had a gray cast to it. The mountains off to his right were still partially steeped in heavy shadow.

He'd driven into Albuquerque many times, through the mountain passes and down—the view had been breathtaking. It still was he thought, but as he followed about a mile from the closest high ridge, flying low, he could see that the view had changed.

He had no idea if Albuquerque had been hit directly, but there had been a firestorm. Perhaps from natural gas? He could see that there were few houses standing; the ground was burned black. Some emergency vehicles were moving on the ground below him. But there was no sign, no huge crater, to indicate that a direct hit had been made on the city.

He found the markers for the airport—a few were still standing. He started to follow them in. "This is Canamerican 747 Flight 601," Rourke droned into the radio. "Calling Albuquerque tower. Do you read me? Over."

He had set the radio to the right frequency for hailing the facility, but there was nothing to answer him but static. Both fists locked on the controls, Rourke whispered, "All right, Mrs. Richards, I'm going to overfly the airport, and we'll see how it looks. After that, I'll have just enough fuel left to set this thing down there or on the desert. So let's make it a good look."

Rourke throttled back on the monster-sized jet engines. The noise roared in his ears as he squinted against the brightness of the sun and scanned the ground. He hauled up on the flaps, and the airport loomed up ahead.

The field—from one end to the other—was a mass of debris. What looked like dozens of planes had been burned on the ground.

"What happened?" Mrs. Richards asked. "A missile?"

"No, I don't think so. I think some kind of accident. Probably somebody like us tried to come in and misjudged the runway. Yeah, see over there?" Rourke pointed far on the starboard side of the plane. "Looks like something rammed a fuel truck and they didn't get the fire in time. Fire-storm of some kind is what it looks like all over the city. So the city shouldn't be hot with radioactivity."

There was the recognizable framework of a huge tank truck, black and gutted, amid the wreckage of a large commercial jet.

"We're not going to land here," Rourke said. He throttled forward and got the nose up, banking as gently as he could to get south of what had been the city. The ruins vanished from beneath them; the ground turned into scrub brush and sand. Rourke throttled down again and slowly played the instruments to get the plane's altitude down. "I don't know exactly how low or how slow I can get this thing and still be able to keep air speed. And if I lose engine power, this thing will fall like a rock. Hit that seat-belt light and get on the PA. Tell the stewardess to get everyone into a crash position."

Rourke scanned the ground. Silently, he prayed that he could have some idea what he was doing. As far as landing went, there was no similarity between the 747 and military fighter aircraft he had flown before. Bringing this down was like playing Russian roulette with all chambers full.

He squinted against the morning sunlight, watching the altimeter, the fuel gauge and the other instruments. He heard Mrs. Richards alert the passengers for a possible crash.

By the time Mrs. Richards had finished the announcement, Rourke was banking the plane gently, having climbed in order to accomplish the maneuver. "I picked out our landing field, Mrs. Richards," he commented. "Nice, flat stretch about five miles long with no frees to speak of, back about twenty-five miles. I'm going around for a try. We can only do it once. I'm letting us run out of fuel to minimize the risk of fire. One other thing I want you to do. Alert the stewardesses that as soon as we get down on the ground, I want everyone out of here as quickly as possible and as far away from the plane as they can. And I want you in a crash position right by the escape chute in the main cabin. You've done great."

"Won't you need me to help?"

"Well," Rourke began, "I don't believe two of us can land this thing any better than one. And you've got a cool head. That's going to be needed if anyone's going to survive after we land. Chances are good the cockpit will get the heaviest impact."

"You mean you'll be killed, and if I don't stay with you, I'll have a better chance of staying alive."

"Yeah, pretty much. Goes back to what we talked about last night. That you opt for life. Anything else is irrational, Mrs. Richards. You don't strike me as an irrational person. And I'd bet that your husband wasn't the kind of guy who'd want you to give up on life."

Rourke brought the plane into another banking maneuver to line up for his final approach. He glanced at Mrs. Richards. She said, "Are you a psychiatrist too, Mr. Rourke?"

"Only the bargain-basement kind," Rourke said, smiling broadly.

"That's the first time I've seen you smile." She rose and started back toward the forward passenger cabin, then turned to him and said, "I hope you make it— and that your wife and children made it too." She leaned down and kissed him on the cheek. Quietly, Rourke said, "Thank you, Mrs. Richards."

As soon as Rourke heard the cockpit cabin door close, he settled himself back in the captain's seat and tightened the lap and shoulder restraints. He fished in the breast pocket of his jacket for his sunglasses to fight the glare from the sand below him. Slowly, he throttled back, stepping down the 747's altitude. The plane was close to the ground now. It raced away beneath the nose of the big jet; it was as if the air speed were a hundred times faster than the readout on the instrument panel. He dropped the landing gear, and the green light indicating that it was locked in place flashed on. He throttled back more. The starboard engines nearly stalled, but he held the speed, skimming less than five hundred feet above the scrub-dotted desert floor.

The 747's nose started to drop, and he brought it up.

The starboard engines almost stalled again, and the altimeter needle started dropping. He punched the PA button and talked into the small microphone attached to the radio headset. "This is Rourke—brace yourselves for impact!"

He tried bringing the nose up, throttled back almost all the way, and let the engines nearly die as the landing gear touched ground, bounced away, and touched again. He throttled forward slightly, using the engine compression to slow the plane as it raced, skipping on the landing gear, across the desert floor. His mike was still open, and he rasped, "We're down but not stopped. Stay in the crash position!"

The plane wasn't slowing as much as he wanted. Rourke stared ahead. The ground dropped off less than a mile away, and he didn't know what was beyond it. He worked the starboard flaps, and the plane started to turn. Mentally, he made the choice. He cut the engines and decided to burn out the brakes. He brought the flaps on both wings all the way up. The plane was starting to slow down, but in front of him was a stand of tall pines. "We're gonna hit," he rasped into the microphone which was inches from his lips. His face was drawn into a tight mask, his lips pulled back, his shoulders set. The brakes held for a moment, then, suddenly the plane lurched, and there was no more pressure.

Rourke could see beyond the stand of pines now. A rock face rose up from the desert floor. Already, the nose of the cockpit was cutting into the trees. He threw his arms up in front of his face and doubled forward. He couldn't see, but the sound was like a thousand chain saws, the pines crashing down on the plane.

The plane lurched and suddenly came to a complete stop. He looked up. The windshields were cracked, shattered, but still holding up. Trees were all around him—pine branches virtually covered the front of the fuselage. He sat for a moment, breathing heavily. Then he fumbled for the microphone.

"This is Rourke. We're down. Now get the hell out of the plane, but don't panic. Everything seems fine." He tossed the headset down, then tore open the seat and shoulder belts and pushed out of the captain's seat.

When he had thrown open the door, he stopped. The portside of the forward cabin's fuselage was almost completely ripped away. A large tree jutted into the cabin, like a can opener. People were screaming, and he knew that others were trapped in the wreckage. As he started back to help them, something on the floor caught his eye.

He looked at it for a moment, then turned away and leaned against the bulkhead. It was the severed head of Mrs. Richards.

Chapter Twenty Six

"We'll be together soon," was all the president could say as his wife and children left his office in the Mt. Lincoln complex. He had tried to tell his wife, without letting his children know. But he couldn't find the words. Bobby's face and his wife's were the last faces he saw, as his family turned down the corridor. Bobby was still holding the spaceship. The president turned to Paul Dorian who was standing in the corridor.

"They've landed?"

"Only in token numbers, Mr. President—and they're pushing the timing on the neutron radiation a little at that. Those cities—like Chicago—are still hot."

"Paul, what about the Eden Project. Did it get off?"

"Yes," Dorian said, his eyes downcast. "Without a hitch, sir."

"Then maybe there is some hope after all. Send in the chief of my Secret Service detail."

"Mr. President, you can't do this."

"I have to—if there's going to be any United States left. It's not a country, a land-mass, Paul. I finally see that. The United States is an idea. And if I don't do this, the idea may well die. I don't have much of a choice, do I?"

The president took the outstretched hand of Paul Dorian, then walked back into his office and sat on the couch. In a moment, the chief of his Secret Service detail, Mike Clemmer, came through the door. "Mike, I've got a favor to ask."

"Anything, Mr. President," Clemmer said, entering the room.

"Take this." He handed Clemmer an envelope with the presidential seal in the upper left corner. "And now, give me your revolver."

Clemmer started to reach under his windbreaker, then stopped.

"That's an order, Mike. There are two letters in the envelope. One is to my wife, the other is to the American people. Thurston Potter knows what to do with them. This is my last order, Mike. Give me your gun."

Clemmer wiped his palms on the sides of his trouser legs and reached under his jacket to his right hip. The president watched as he produced a short-barreled, shiny revolver. "I don't know much about guns, Mike. Always wanted to try them, but never had the time. Does yours have a safety catch?"

"No, sir. Revolvers don't. Mr. President, you can't. I can't let you."

"You've got to, Mike. If I stay alive, the Russians will find me and use me. If I die, there will be no government left to capitulate, and free Americans will go on fighting until there is a government again—another elected government that will throw the Soviets out. If they get me, it's all over for all of us."

"But Mr. President—they'll never get into Mt. Lincoln."

"You know that's not true," the president said. "And if we're totally cut off, they've got a capitulation anyway. But if the American people know I'm gone, then the Soviets—no matter what they do—can't lie to the American people that the United States has surrendered. It's the only way. Now, give me the gun."

The president looked away from Mike Clemmer and extended his right hand, lighting a cigarette with his left.

He felt the heavy steel object in his hand, then heard the footsteps across the carpet. When he looked up, Mike Clemmer was gone. The president looked into the empty hallway through his open door.

The president of the United States dragged heavily on the cigarette and held the smoke in his lungs. He glanced at the picture of his wife and children on the coffee table in front of him, then looked straight into the stubby muzzle of the revolver. He touched the first finger of his right hand to the trigger . . .

Chapter Twenty Seven

Sarah Rourke turned on her heel and took the .45 automatic from the waist-band of her blue jeans. The corners of her mouth raised into a smile and her green eyes lost their hard set. "Ron Jenkins," she said. The man she stared at was a familiar one, the retired Army sergeant who owned the next farm. He rode a tall Appaloosa gelding. She knew the horse well. On a bay, behind him, was his wife, Carla, and riding behind her on the same horse was their ten year old girl, Millie.

"My wife and me—we was gettin' ready to clear out on horseback here, then we heard the explosion over your place this morning and I said to Carla, "Betchya Sarah Rourke's got some problems—John probably ain't home."

Sarah slipped the .45 automatic back into her waistband, gestured with the same hand toward the smoldering ruins of the house and said, "I guess you'd call them brigands or something. They wanted to rob us and—well, you know," Sarah said, turning away from the Jenkins family and looking back to the tack she was adjusting on her chestnut colored mare. The white mare with the black mane and tail and four black stockings—John's horse—was already saddled and the gear tied on. She finished adjusting the latigo strap on her own horse and turned back to the Jenkins. "Thanks for coming to see about us," she said quietly.

"You want we should all ride together? I'm taking my wife and daughter up into the mountains. Not far, but should be safer," Ron Jenkins said.

"Come with us, Sarah," Carla Jenkins said, leaning forward in her saddle.

Sarah wiped the palms of her hands on the legs of her jeans, then glanced at Michael and Annie standing beside the barn. Carla Jenkins talked too much, and Ron Jenkins didn't talk enough—and their daughter Millie was a brat, Sarah recalled. But she looked at her children again. "I guess there's safety in num-bers," she said. "I thank you for coming for us. I know it was out of your way. We'll be happy to come with you. I'm sure we can all help each other. I'm almost through here. I just have one thing to do."

"I'll help your children get mounted up," Ron Jenkins said. "On your husband's horse—the white one?"

"Yes—please," Sarah said, smiling. She walked back to the barn doorway and gave each of the children a nudge, then reached into her canvas purse and took a pen and the checkbook. She tore off a check and almost laughed as she found herself starting to write "void" across the front. They were all void now, she realized. She dropped to her knees on the ground and, using the checkbook to steady her hand, wrote:

"My Dearest John, You were right. I don't know if you're still alive. I'm telling myself and the children that you survived. We are fine. The chickens died overnight, but I don't think it was radiation. No one is sick. The Jenkins family came by and we're heading toward the mountains with them. You can find us from the retreat. I'm telling myself that you will find us. Maybe it will take a long time, but we won't give up hope. Don't you. The children love you. Annie has been good, Michael is more of a little man than we'd thought. Some thieves came by and Michael saved my life. We weren't hurt. Hurry. Always, Sarah"

She slipped the note inside a plastic sandwich bag—from Michael's lunch the last day he'd been in school. There was a nail already driven into the inside of the barn door, and she stuck the plastic bag over it, took one last look at the note, took the bag down and took out the check again. At the bottom, in larger letters, she scrawled, "I love you, John," put the note back in the bag and hung it back on the nail.

Snatching up her black canvas purse, she turned on her heel and ran toward her horse, then climbed into the saddle.

"You ready, Sarah?" Ron Jenkins asked.

Sarah Rourke looked at the Jenkins family, then at her children, then pressed her heels gently against her horse's flanks. She held the reins from John's horse which carried Michael and Ann, in her left hand. As they started from the yard, she looked back. The ruins of the house were still smoking. But her attention focused on the barn door, the note to her husband nailed to the inside. Silently, she prayed that he was alive to read it.

"Come on, Tildie," she whispered to the mare between her legs.

Chapter Twenty Eight

John Rourke leaned back against a rock and stared at the wrecked airplane two hundred yards away. He closed his eyes, and he wanted to put his hands over his ears to shut out the moaning of the injured passengers—the ones he'd worked through the long day to save.

"Mr. Rourke—coffee?"

He opened his eyes. The stewardess—the same one who had helped him at the beginning—was standing beside him, a coffee cup in her hand.

"Yeah, thanks," he said.

"I don't believe the way you were able to get everybody out, Mr. Rourke, then go back for the things in the cargo hold. You're a real, live hero."

Rourke smiled at the woman. "Well, going back into the cargo hold was pure selfishness. I needed the stuff I had there."

"Those?"

Rourke followed her eyes to the twin stainless Detonics .45's in the holster across his shoulders. "Yeah—and the other ones, too. I'm going to have to go into town for some medical help—if I can find it. There isn't much more I can do for most of the people who were injured. And when I leave you people, you may need to defend yourselves. And I need to defend myself when I try making it into Albuquerque."

"Defend ourselves? From what? Surely, no one—"

Rourke cut her off. "Let me ask you a question," he said. "Would you have felt comfortable walking around in a high-crime area in Atlanta last night? Or any night?"

"Well—no."

"How about Chicago, New York, Los Angeles?"

"Well—certainly I wouldn't have, but—"

"Now, that's with police, civil courts, the whole shot of civilization. What about with no police, no courts, no laws—no civilization?"

"But—"

"People who'd hit you over the head to steal your money when there might be a cop looking will kill you to steal your food, your medical supplies, your ammunition—when their lives depend on getting it. You understand? Since last night, in almost any area you can think of, there is no law, no protection. The only recourse you have is yourself, or someone who cares enough about you to put himself on the line."

"Is that why you're going for help, Mr. Rourke?" the stewardess asked.

"Somebody has to," Rourke grunted. "I'm going to leave you in charge—with a gun. That Canadian businessman who was sitting next to me—what's his name?"

"Mr. Quentin?"

"Yeah, well he said that he shoots. I'll leave him a gun, too—two of them. If somebody shows up and starts acting funny," shoot first and ask questions afterward. Got it? I'm taking about five or six people in with me—just in case we can't get help to come out here, we'll be able to bring enough stuff back to do something. I make it twenty, maybe twenty-five miles into Albuquerque. We'll be there by dawn. Be back by tomorrow night, late, probably. So just hold out, huh?"

Rourke took the stewardess aside and showed her how to work the Colt Python .357, then left it with her. He gave his CAR-15 rifle to his florid-faced exseatmate, along with the snub-nosed metalifed Colt Lawman .357 revolver, reminding him the stewardess was in charge. Among the survivors, he found five men strong enough and willing to accompany him on foot to Albuquerque. He let one of the five carry his Steyr-Mannlicher bolt-action rifle. It was cool on the desert with night falling, and he pulled a sweater on over his shirt and the Allessi shoulder rig with his Detonics .45s, then pulled his sportcoat back on over the sweater. He started from the camp with his group. He heard the stewardess running after him.

"Mr. Rourke! I thought you and the other men could use these." She handed him a paper bag.

"Sandwiches?"

"Uh-huh."

"Thoughtful, Miss . . .?" Rourke had still not bothered to learn the young woman's name.

"Sandy Benson," she said, smiling.

"You have a pretty smile, Sandy," Rourke said, then turned and started away from the impromptu camp.

He glanced at his watch, then at the hazy moon. The Rolex on his wrist read eight P.M. Shifting his right shoulder under the water bottle suspended there on a borrowed trouser belt, he looked at the five men with him and then at the open ground in front of them. He guessed they would make four or five miles an hour. With rest stops, they'd be in Albuquerque by sunrise or before.

He walked with the five men in silence for the first hour, making a better pace than he'd thought they would. Then he called a rest stop. The five sat by themselves and made no move to talk with him. He watched them for a while, then tried remembering their names. One was O'Toole. Another, Rubenstein. Then there was Phillips. He couldn't remember the last two names.

One of the men—one of the two whose names he didn't remember—said, suddenly, "Are you really coming back, Rourke?"

"That's what I told everybody," Rourke answered quietly.

"Are you for real?"

"Why shouldn't I?" Rourke asked.

"Well, most of those people back there are dying, except for the stewardess you left your rifle with, and the Canadian guy and a few others, maybe."

"Left my rifle with the Canadian. I left the stewardess a revolver," Rourke corrected. "Don't you think we owe it to the people back there to help?"

"What about us?"

"Well, what about us?"

The one who had been talking started to get to his feet. "Well," he said, walking toward Rourke, "I say we don't."

Rourke stood, his back aching. "Then, just don't go back," he said. "We can get along okay without you."

"Yeah," the man said, stopping less than a yard from Rourke. "But that isn't the point. With your guns, we'd stand a better chance."

"I can see where that's true," Rourke said, looking away from the man a moment and nodding his head. "And you figure you need all the help you can get. Like my guns. Right?"

"Right."

"Not right," Rourke said softly, and his left fist hammered forward and into the man's stomach. At the same time, his right knee came up and connecting with the side of the man's jaw. Already, both of Rourke's hands had snatched one of the Detonics .45's from the shoulder holsters. Rourke took a step back. One of the other four men had the stock of Rourke's SSG sniper rifle to his shoulder. Rourke shouted, "You might get off one shot—but while you're working that bolt action, I'll kill all of you unless that first shot is a good one. Your move. I said my piece."

He thought it was Rubenstein, but wasn't sure. The man stepped away from the other three, hands in the air, saying, "Hey—wait. I'm not with them."

A second man, carrot-red hair in his eyes, stepped beside Rubenstein. It was O'Toole. "Me neither!"

Keeping one of the guns trained on Rubenstein and O'Toole, Rourke shouted, "What about it?" to the other two men. He could hear the man he'd decked starting to groan.

The man holding Rourke's rifle started to lower the gun from his shoulder.

"Don't drop it—set it down slowly," Rourke whispered. "Rubenstein," he rasped, hoping he was matching the name to the right face. The man who'd first broken away took a step toward him. "Pick up my rifle. Grab it by the barrel and come here and stretch it out to me. Be quick about it."

Rourke watched as Rubenstein walked over, picked up the rifle by the muzzle end, then started toward him. Rourke shoved the Detonics from his left hand into his belt, reaching out with his free hand and grasping the stock of the rifle. He slid the gun through his hand, catching it forward of the trigger guard along the front stock, then slipped his left arm between the rifle and the sling and hauled the synthetic stocked bolt action onto his left shoulder.

The man he'd knocked down was groaning louder now, and Rourke stepped back from him. Then, looking at the four men still standing, Rourke said slowly, "Now—if I were smart, I'd kill all of you right now and save myself headaches later on. Once we get into Albuquerque, anybody who wants to come into this with me and go back for the rest of the passengers can. Anybody who doesn't, just stay away from me. But if you split and if I ever see you again, I'll kill you. Now, you two," and Rourke gestured toward Rubenstein and O'Toole. "Pick up this guy and get him walking. We're moving out, and all you guys are staying in front of me. One wrong move from anybody and he gets a bullet—maybe two just for luck. Questions?"

None of the four men said anything. Rubenstein and O'Toole walked forward slowly and started helping the fifth man off the ground. "All right—let's start walkin'," Rourke said.

Chapter Twenty Nine

Rourke stood in the middle of the square; in front of him—miraculously, still standing—was the oldest church in the American southwest. Around it, much of the rest of Albuquerque's old town was gutted and burned. He glanced down to the Rolex on his wrist. It was almost four A.M., and the sun would not be up for more than three hours. There were no lights, except for lights from inside the church, and Rourke assumed these had to be Coleman lamps or candles. Whole streets had ripped apart when the fire-storm had hit natural gas lines. There was no electricity.

Rourke shivered under his sweater and coat. Shifting the rifle from his shoulder, he stood there a moment, staring at the old church. He remembered taking Sarah and Michael there once, several years ago. Michael had enjoyed playing in the old town cul-de-sacs, watching the Indians selling their jewelry along the square. Sarah had wanted a rug from one of the shops, but for some reason which Rourke couldn't remember now, they hadn't purchased it.

There were no people on the street, but he could hear the howling of dogs. Rourke turned and glanced at the five men with him, standing together to his left. "Well," he said. "I guess here's where we part company—at least those who want to. Looks from here like that Catholic Church is probably being used as a shelter. Anybody's who's not coming with me back to the plane, can split here. I'm going to check that shelter after I take care of a couple of things, then I'm going to find the closest thing to a hospital." He lit a cigar, then said, "Anybody coming with me, step over here."

None of the five men moved for a moment. Then Rubenstein—a smallish man with a receding hairline and wire framed glasses—stepped away from the other four and walked toward Rourke. "What about you, O'Toole?" Rourke said through a cloud of cigar smoke.

"No. I don't want to go back," O'Toole said. "I don't know if I'm hanging in with them, either, but I'm not going back to the plane."

"Suit yourself—and good luck," Rourke added.

Turning to Rubenstein, Rourke said, "Well, friend. Let's go." Without waiting for a reply, Rourke started across the fire-scorched square, picking his way over the large gouges in the pavement and away from the church.

He heard Rubenstein, beside him saying, "Where are we going, Mr. Rourke?"

"It's John. What's your first name?"

"Paul."

"Well, Paul, Albuquerque is a town where a lot of people were interested in prospecting. Geology, things like that. So I'm looking to find a geological equipment shop, where there might be a Geiger counter. I want to see how much radiation we've taken. And then, we get back to the plane. I want to check out the rest of us."

Rubenstein walked silently for a while, then asked, "Tell me, John, what're you going to do then—after we help those people back there?"

Rourke turned and looked at him, "Well, going back across the country. See, my wife, Sarah, and our two children. They're back in Georgia."

"But all those missiles that were going off around the Mississippi River— that whole area between here and Georgia is going to be just a huge desert, a big crater."

Rourke said slowly, "I've thought of that. Here, turn down here." He moved onto the ruins of a side street. "There were a lot of little stores down here, I remember."

"I never been to Albuquerque before," Rubenstein said.

"It was a nice town," Rourke said, his voice low. "But, anyway, I'll get back to Georgia—maybe work my way down through Mexico then up along the Gulf Coast. I'll have to play it by ear."

"What if they're dead when you get there?"

Rourke stopped in mid-stride and turned to Rubenstein. "You married?"

"No, I have a mother and father in St. Petersburg, Florida."

"Are you going back for them?"

"I hadn't thought about it. I don't know."

"You got anyplace else to go, anything else to do?"

"No, I guess not."

125

"Neither have I," Rourke said. "I'm going on the idea that my wife and children are still alive. I'm going to look for them. And if they're not home—we had a farm in a rural part of the state—and I don't find hard evidence that they're dead, I'll keep on looking."

"But aren't we all gonna die?" Rubenstein said, his voice starting to crack.

"All of humanity wiped out? I'm not plannin' on it." At that, Rourke turned and continued walking, stopping a few yards further down what was left of the street in front of a partially burned building.

"Well—look at that," Rourke said, pointing up at the sign above it.

" 'Geological Supplies,' " Rubenstein read aloud.

"Yeah, looks like." Rourke pushed against the door—all the glass was broken out—and the door moved in a foot. Reaching under his coat, he grabbed the Detonics from under his left arm and stepped through the door frame, Rubenstein close behind him.

"This place is in ruins."

"Looks like, but let's see," Rourke said. The floor of what had once been the store was covered with charred pieces of wood, broken glass, some half-burned small cardboard boxes. The fire, Rourke guessed, had burned through quickly.

The back portion of the shop was relatively untouched except for dark scorch-marks on the walls.

"Jees," Rubenstein muttered.

"What's the matter?"

"I tripped—this place is as dark as a closet."

"Just have to get your eyes accustomed," Rourke said quietly. "Close your eyes and count to ten, then open them. There's moonlight from outside- enough to see by if you look close.

"It looks like some sort of storeroom, back there, Rubenstein," Rourke said.

"Where? That door?"

"Yeah. Watch your step now," Rourke said. Then he picked his way across the rubble on the floor.

"It smells funny in here," Rubenstein said.

"Well, it isn't gas. More like burned flesh," Rourke said matter-of-factly.

"Burned what?"

"People, Rubenstein. Come on." He tried the doorknob, but the door didn't budge. Taking a step back, he raised his right leg and kicked. His foot smashed hard against the lock and the door fell inward.

"Just like in the movies," Rubenstein remarked.

Rourke turned and looked at Rubenstein, saying nothing. The storage room, high-ceilinged and narrow, was darker than the store had been. Rourke waited in the doorway, letting his eyes become accustomed to the dimness.

"You must see real well in the dark," Rubenstein said.

"I do. But it has its disadvantages. If I don't wear sunglasses when I'm outside during the day, the brightness gives me headaches—bothers my eyes." He started into the storeroom. "Here, just a second," he said, and in a moment there was a soft clicking sound then a light. "Flashlight—the guy must have sold them. I had to find batteries for them. Here," Rourke said, handing the flashlight to Rubenstein, "take this—I'll fix another one for myself."

"Isn't this stealing? I mean, couldn't we get shot as looters?"

"Yeah, we could," Rourke said, tightening his grip on the flashlight and flicking it on. "Not a very good flashlight," Rourke commented, flashing the anglehead light around the room. He stopped the beam at the high shelves at the back of the room.

"Look! What do you want for free?" Rubenstein commented.

"Yeah, I suppose you're right," Rourke said. "Give me a leg up so I can get to that top shelf."

"What leg up?" Rubenstein said.

"Here," Rourke said. "Put your hands together like that." Rourke put his right foot in Rubenstein's palms, then pushed himself up on the shelves.

"For a lanky guy, you're sure heavy," Rubenstein gasped.

Rourke stretched to reach the shelf, got a grip on a box, then slid down to the floor.

"What is that?"

"A Geiger counter. Looks like the last one he had. I have to put some batteries in it." He dropped to his knees, ripped open the box, then produced a dark-bladed knife and praised at the cowling on the machine.

"What kind of a knife is that?"

"Sting IA black chrome—it's a boot knife," Rourke said absently. "Hand me some of those batteries from the shelf up there—the big ones."

Rubenstein handed Rourke a half-dozen batteries. Rourke took what he needed and said, "Hold onto the rest of them. You might find a couple more flashlights and get them working. See if there's anything else we could use. A couple of good-sized hunting knives wouldn't be a bad idea. And see if you can find some compasses. Oh—the knives— look for thick blades rather than long ones."

"Gotcha," Rubenstein said.

Rubenstein left the storeroom and Rourke finished placing the batteries, then replaced the cowling on the Geiger counter. He flicked the on switch and took the microphone-like attachment and swept it across his clothes. He watched the Roentgen reading, stripped off his jacket, then took another reading. He stood and stripped off the rest of his clothes and weapons, taking a reading on each item. His guns, the holsters, his knife, even the sweater he'd taken from his luggage in the cargo compartment—all were normal. The clothes he'd worn in the cockpit were reading high. He ran the counter over his skin and the reading was normal. His watch—the Rolex he habitually wore—was reading too high. He took it off and took another reading. His body was normal. He picked up his guns and knife and left the clothes in the storeroom, then walked back into the store, squinting as Rubenstein's light flashed across his face.

"You're naked!"

"Yeah, aren't I though," Rourke said. "I took a Geiger counter reading. My clothes and everything must have gotten contaminated up in the cockpit. But my sweater, my guns—everything from the cargo hold—were fine. I even had to ditch my watch."

"That was a Rolex wasn't it? That's about fifteen hundred bucks!"

"A radioactive watch won't due me much good. Besides, I've got another one back at the plane," Rourke said. "Here," he said, "I'm gonna sweep your clothes with the counter. You might be hot, too."

Rourke checked Rubenstein with the wand of the Geiger counter and stepped back. "You should strip. Your clothes are contaminated."

"But I can't run around naked."

"Your choice, friend," Rourke said. "Would you rather get radiation poisoning?"

Rubenstein started to undress. Once the man was naked, Rourke ran the Geiger counter over him. "Get rid of your watch," he said.

"Sure," Rubenstein said, "You threw away a Rolex—I can throw away a Timex. What the hell, huh?"

"Come on," Rourke said. "That next block over looked pretty much untouched by the fire—maybe we can find a clothing store or something."

Rourke started out of the store, Rubenstein behind him. "Jees—its cold."

"Here," Rourke said, and he tossed Rubenstein his sweater. "And watch your feet."

The double shoulder holster across his back, the rifle slung from his shoulder, the Geiger counter in his left hand and the flashlight in his right, Rourke started down the street toward the next block, aware of his nakedness only because of the night air. His main concern—and he began walking more rapidly—was the howling sound some distance behind him.

"What's that noise?" Rubenstein asked, a few feet behind Rourke.

"Wild dogs—running in a pack," Rourke said, his voice even.

"A pack of hungry wild dogs, huh?" Rubenstein said. "And here we are, meat on the hoof, huh?"

"You've got the idea, Rubenstein," Rourke said, smiling. "And, speak of the devil."

Rourke stopped and turned, Rubenstein beside him now. The howling was louder, and at the end of the street in plain sight, less than fifty yards from Rourke and Rubenstein, stood six dogs. Five German shepherds and one Doberman.

"My God," Rubenstein muttered.

"The Lord helps those who help themselves, doesn't he?" Rourke said, snatching one of the Detonics pistols into his right hand. His knife was clipped to his shoulder rig, but his left hand was crowded with the Geiger counter, the flashlight, and a bag of spare ammo he had taken from the store. "Here, hold my stuff," Rourke rasped.

"You just gonna stand here?"

"Yeah," he said. "Until they come at us in a run. Then I'm going to shoot them. Here—take the rifle in case I miss one of 'em."

"Oh," Rubenstein said, taking Rourke's SSG. "I never shot a gun in my life."

"First time for everything. Bet you never walked down the street naked before either."

"Well, yeah," Rubenstein said.

Rourke smiled, snatching the second Detonics from its holster.

The dogs started edging forward. "How good a shot are you?" Rubenstein asked, nervously.

"Not bad," Rourke said. "Better than average, I guess," he added.

"Oh. You're not bad. Better than average," Rubenstein said, laughing. "Well, listen. I'm glad of that."

The dogs started breaking into a loping run now, their speed increasing as they approached.

"Must be pretty hungry to attack people who look like they can defend themselves," Rourke said slowly, raising the Detonics stainless .45 in his right hand, his left hand with the matching gun still hanging limp at his side.

"Must be," Rubenstein said, taking a step back.

The nearest of the dogs—the largest German shepherd—was thirty feet away when Rourke fired. The hollow point round caught the animal square in the chest and it dropped.

Already, Rourke had the second Detonics raised and cocked. He squeezed the trigger. The bullet cut into the second of the German shepherds. The animal yelped once, ran a few paces, and fell. With the pistol in his right hand, Rourke sighted on the Doberman, then fired.

"Missed," Rourke mumbled, firing then with the pistol in his left hand, catching the Doberman and dropping it instantly.

The pack was less than fifteen feet away now, and Rourke lowered both guns to midway between his shoulders and waist and fired, first the one in his right hand, then, as he brought it back on line, the one in his left. The hot brass burned against his naked chest and thighs. He fired both .45's simultaneously at the last dog, dropping it in mid-air as it sprang toward him. Then he let both pistols drop to his sides.

He took a step forward, then turned to listen to Rubenstein who was saying, "That was spectacular—I never saw anything like that in my life. It was like a movie or something. You would have made one hell of a great cowboy in the old west, John Rourke."

Rourke stooped over the nearest dog, studying it. Then he stood, fished in the bag for spare magazines for his pistols and reloaded, saying to Rubenstein, "That dog has rabies. Watch out for cats, dogs, anything. We gotta get out of here, soon."

Without another word, they started down the street in their original direction. Rubenstein had slung the rifle across his shoulders.

On the next block, Rourke stopped, staring up and down the street, then pointing. "Over there. We'll see if there's anything left—might have been looted."

He started walking toward the clothing store, Rubenstein behind him. There was no glass in the windows; it had blown inward. Rourke glanced down the street. There was a huge hole where, apparently, a gas main had ruptured. Beyond that, at the end of the block, all the buildings were burned.

"Why are some of the buildings left, some only partway burned do you suppose?" Rubenstein asked.

"A fire-storm is a funny thing—it feeds on itself, builds its own winds. There's no logic to it. That's why they're so dangerous. Probably," and Rourke— cautiously because of his bare feet— stepped through the smashed glass door, "when that plane hit the gasoline tanker truck at the airport, the city was pretty much evacuated. May have been expecting a Soviet missile to be targeted on them. No one to put out the fire, got into the gas system and gas mains blew— then a firestorm. It must have burned itself out fast though."

"Here," Rubenstein said. "Take your flashlight."

"Thanks," Rourke muttered, shining the beam along the length of the store. The merchandise seemed untouched. "Help yourself," Rourke said over his shoulder, starting toward a table loaded with Levis.

After ten minutes both men were dressed again— jeans, shirts, boots. And each took a jacket.

Rourke stopped by the cash register and walked behind the counter, going into the smashed display case and snatching a handful of Timex watches. "Here," he shouted, tossing a couple of the watches to Rubenstein, then putting two on his left wrist.

"Got any idea what time it is?" Rubenstein asked.

"Doesn't really matter anymore. A watch is just a way of keeping track of elapsed time. When the sun rises, it'll be about seven. Grab yourself a wide-brimmed hat, Paul," he added. "That sun on the desert'll be strong tomorrow.

Rourke snatched a pair of dark-lensed aviator sunglasses and tried them on, then found a dark gray Stetson in his size.

As they left, he said, "Let's head for that church and then find the nearest hospital."

Chapter Thirty

"I never wore a cowboy hat before," Rubenstein said. "Except when I was a kid."

Rourke turned as he started opening the door into the church. "Is that a fact? Come on."

Rourke stepped inside, Rubenstein behind him. Then both men turned back toward the door. Rubenstein started coughing. "My God!"

"Yeah, ain't it though," Rourke said, turning back to look down the church's long main aisle and toward the altar. The smell of burnt flesh was strong. The pews had been converted into beds—people were lined one after the other, head to head along them.

Rourke started up the aisle. The pews were jammed with burn victims, as were the floors. He picked his way past the people in the aisles. A few were sitting up. They had open, festering sores on their beet-red faces. Many of them had their eyes bandaged. There were nuns—about six or seven—moving slowly about the church, and near the front of the church he saw a priest. He walked toward the man, tapped him on the shoulder.

The priest was gently washing the face of a little girl. The hair on the left side of her head was burned away. Her face was a mass of blisters. "Father?" Rourke said.

The priest turned toward him then. Rourke studied the priest's face. He was dark—apparently Chicano. It looked like he hadn't shaved for several days. "Father, my name is Rourke. My friend here and I are from a commercial jetliner that crashed about twenty-five miles south of here. I need to find a hospital, some medical—" but he stopped.

The priest's eyes were almost smiling, but not quite. Rourke whispered, "*This* is the hospital?"

"Yes. All the hospitals were destroyed in the firestorm. We here are doing what we can, but there must be thousands out there in the ruins—like this one. There is no one to help your people on the plane."

"What about medical supplies?" Rourke asked.

"Water—and that is running out. We make bandages from what we can."

"I see," Rourke said slowly, starting to stand. Then he leaned over the little girl. He said, "Are you a doctor, Father?"

"We have no doctor."

Rourke looked back to Rubenstein, and Rubenstein nodded, his face set in a grim mask.

"You do now—at least for a few hours. I'm a doctor."

"God has heard me," the priest said, crossing himself and smiling.

"Well, I can't say about that."

He started working then, until sunrise, then noon, and long into the afternoon. As soon as he thought he'd seen every patient, another was brought in.

The little girl died at noon. There were no drugs, no pain killers and Rourke realized bitterly that most of the more serious cases would end in death. But at least he had been able to help some of them. As night started to fall, he checked one of the worst cases again. The man was dead. Rourke covered his sticky, raw face with a sheet, then stood. Rubenstein was helping the priest move one of the dead, a woman, into the courtyard behind the church.

Rourke followed them, stopping just outside the door. There were dozens of bodies in the yard, seventy-five or more, Rourke judged. Rourke walked over to the priest. "Father, I'm going to have to get back to the plane now."

"Yes. I have been waiting all afternoon for you to say this. I knew you would have to return to the airplane. May God go with you."

"You'd better get those bodies buried, Father. Soon."

"I will do what I can."

"Move them and burn them, then," Rourke advised.

The priest stared at Rourke. "They will be buried. I know most of these people. They were Catholic. They must be buried as Catholics."

"If I could, I'd hang around and help," Rourke said quietly. "I'm sorry."

"You have helped—and God bless you for it."

Rourke took the priest's outstretched hand, then turned to go.

"I'm coming, John," Rubenstein said.

Rourke turned to him, holding his hat in his hands, saying, "After all this time, I don't know what we'll find out there, Paul."

"I know that," the smaller man said. "I'm going with you anyway."

Rourke just nodded, turned, and started toward the main doors, Rubenstein behind him.

It was dark again by the time Rourke and Rubenstein reached the edge of the city. The howling of the wild dogs in the distance grew louder with the falling darkness.

Much of the residential section here had not been burned, but was deserted. "Where d'you suppose everyone went?" Rubenstein said.

"Up there," said Rourke, pointing toward the mountains on the other side of the city. "For some reason, whenever there's disaster, people always think of going to the mountains. Santa Fe is probably a giant refugee center by now. Doesn't look like there were any hits up there, either."

"Why don't we go to Santa Fe for help, then?"

"Too far to walk, and if the town is still functioning, I'd guess they don't have any doctors, nurses, or medical supplies to spare."

"How come you're a doctor but you run around with guns?"

"That's a long story."

"I got the time," Rubenstein said.

"Well, briefly, I studied to be a doctor, went all through college and medical school, even interned. But then I started watching what was happening in the world and said to myself that as a doctor, all I'd be able to do would be to patch things up for other people. Maybe in the CIA or something like that, I thought, I could keep things from needing to be patched up for a while longer. After a few years in covert operations, down in Latin America, mostly, I saw that wasn't possible. I'd always been into guns—hunting, the outdoors, the whole nine yards. Started getting interested in survivalism. I was a weapons expert already, found myself writing articles and books on it, started getting into the technical side of survival. Wrote about that, too. Because of my degree, I wound up doing a lot of seminars on survival medicine, stuff like that. I traveled all around the United States, parts of Latin America, the Mideast, Europe—teaching survivalism, weapons training. Anyway, here I am."

They walked on in silence for a few minutes, then Rourke stopped Rubenstein as they passed a house on their left. It seemed totally intact. There was a garage at the end of a long driveway, the door closed all the way.

"Look at that," Rourke said, "and see if you're thinking what I'm thinking."

He didn't wait for Rubenstein to reply, but started sprinting toward the garage, up the driveway. He stopped at the garage door and tried it. Locked.

Reaching under his leather jacket, he snatched one of the Detonics pistols from its shoulder holster. "Now I've got a lock I'm *gonna* shoot—get out of the way," he said.

He aimed at the lock and fired once. The lock and most of the handle fell away.

"Go find something to pry at this door with," Rourke said.

In a moment, Rubenstein was back, but empty handed.

"What's the matter?"

"I found something better than a prybar. The side door was unlocked."

"Did you look inside?"

"Yeah. The prettiest '57 Chevy you ever saw. It's up on blocks, but the tires are there."

Rourke followed Rubenstein into the garage. A tarpaulin was draped half over the gleaming fire-engine red and chrome vintage car. "Look for some gas," Rourke almost whispered.

Ten minutes later, they had found three two-gallon gas cans and were beginning to put the wheels on the car. Working now on the last wheel, Rourke said, "Here," then handed Rubenstein one of his pistols. "Take this and look around the block. See if you can find any more gas. That's the gun I used on the door. It's only got five rounds left in it. If I hear you shoot, I'll come running."

Rourke tightened the last of the lug nuts, then started working on the garage door, pulling the chains taut and pushing up until he had released the locking mechanism. He slid the overhead door up and clear of the frame, then walked back to the Chevy. He searched under the front seat and found the ignition key. Then he slid into the front seat and put the key in the ignition. He got out again, took the one water jug he'd brought from the church for himself and Rubenstein to use and checked the battery. He had to pour most of the water into it. He opened the radiator cap—the radiator seemed full when he shone his flashlight inside and he muttered, "Thank you."

Getting back behind the wheel, Rourke tried the ignition. The car groaned a few times. He smashed his fist against the steering wheel. If the battery were dead, it was hopeless. He turned when he heard a sound at the side door. It was Rubenstein.

"I found one more can of gas next to a power mower down the street."

"Good," Rourke muttered. Then, "If this battery doesn't turn this over, you can go out and check for a battery and tools to change it with. Keep your fingers crossed," he added.

He took the key out of the ignition, looked at it and whispered, "Come on baby—this'll be the ride of your life."

He put the key into the lock and turned the ignition. The engine coughed and then roared as he stepped on the gas pedal.

"Yahoo!" Rubenstein shouted. Rourke looked up at him, squinted his eyes against the flashlight he held. "You're takin' that cowboy hat awful serious, aren't you?" Then, "Come on, Paul, pour in that gas and let's get out of here."

The smell of exhaust fumes was thick in the garage, despite both open doors, by the time Rubenstein threw down the empty gas container and ran around the front of the two-door hardtop and climbed in beside Rourke. Rourke looked over at him and smiled. "Let me guess. You've never stolen a car before—or ridden in a '57 Chevy? Right?"

"Yeah," Rubenstein said. "How'd you know?"

"Intuition," Rourke laughed, hauling the big long-throw gearshift into first. "Intuition."

The needle on the speedometer was bouncing near twenty as Rourke slowed at the end of the long driveway. He let up on the clutch again and made a hard left into the street, sliding the stick back into second as he reached the end of the block, then cutting a hard right onto what had been a main street. He raced through the street, then turned onto one of the major arteries.

"You just ran a—" Rubenstein started, but then fell silent, smiling to himself.

"I don't know about you," Rourke said, "but right now I'd be happy if a cop pulled me over for a ticket." He glanced at Rubenstein and the smaller man nodded.

A moment later, Rubenstein said, "Hey—this thing's got a tape deck."

"Wonderful," Rourke said. "Check the glove compartment and see if he's got any tapes."

"One," Rubenstein said a moment later, then inserted the cartridge.

As the music began, the men looked at each other. "The Beach Boys?" Rourke said.

"You gotta admit," Rubenstein said, touching the dashboard, "the music goes with the car."

Chapter Thirty One

Sandy Benson hitched up the skirt of her stewardess uniform and climbed over the rock outcropping, then edged along the large flat rock, stopping and holding her breath to listen. She didn't hear anything. After a moment, she whispered, "Mr. Quentin, are you out there?"

"Shhh," he hissed. "Up here."

She looked to the top of the large, flat rock, then climbed back along it and over the rough outcropping again. Squinting in the darkness, she could just barely make out his silhouette. "Mr. Quentin?"

"I'm coming down," he whispered. She could hear him shuffling toward her, and, soon, he was close enough so that she could make out his features.

As the Canadian approached her, Rourke's CAR-15 slung from his right shoulder, she asked, "Any sign of them, Mr. Quentin?"

"No—not of Rourke or of the people on the motorcycles."

"I wish he'd hurry," she said.

"I don't know much about Rourke," Quentin said, leaning back against the rock, "but he struck me as somebody who'd do his best. He'll be back. But I can't say I liked the look of some of those men he took with him."

"Neither did I," the stewardess whispered, half to herself. Talking louder then, she asked, "Do you think there was any help in Albuquerque. According to what he said, he thought there had been a fire-storm there—wasn't much left of the town."

"I don't know," Quentin said. "I guess all we can hold out for is that Rourke gets here with some help before that motorcycle gang comes back. I counted twenty or more, all of them with rifles or shotguns. And I know they spotted the plane."

"What could they be waiting for?" the girl said, suddenly shaking from the desert's evening chill.

"I don't know," Quentin said. "I hunt, do some target shooting. But I never fired a gun at a person in my life. So I sure can't figure what makes people like that tick. Maybe they were just getting out of Albuquerque and are out to protect themselves. Or maybe not—I don't know."

Sandy shook her head, staring into the darkness. Suddenly, she touched Quentin's arm, whispering, "I hear something."

"I'll go back up and take a look," he said.

"No!" she hissed, holding his arm more tightly. "It's the sound of motorcycles—lots of them. Listen!"

Quentin turned and stared off into the darkness. "You're right. They're coming back."

"We've got to get to the plane!" Sandy Benson stood and started to run back.

Glancing over her shoulder, she saw Quentin following her. She had left Rourke's big revolver beside her purse, back at the camp.

As she rounded a great outcropping rock and headed along the periphery of a stand of pines, she could see the bonfire from the camp where the passengers were, and well beyond that, the silhouette of the abandoned airplane.

She tripped, felt herself falling, and threw her hands in front of her to break the fall. She felt a hand at her elbow and almost screamed, then looked up and saw Quentin beside her. As she started back to her feet, she heard a loud series of bangs.

She turned and stared at Quentin. "My God— those are shots!" Then she broke into a dead run toward the camp, Quentin at her heels.

*****

"You know," Rourke said, "you've played that tape all the way through—twice now."

Rubenstein laughed. It was the first time Rourke had heard him laugh out loud. The smaller man pulled the tape from the deck, then said, "I know this sounds horrible, with all that's happened—I mean, World War Three began two days ago. But here I am, wearing a cowboy hat, riding in a fire-engine red '57 Chevy, out to rescue some people trapped in the desert. Two days ago, I was a junior editor with a trade magazine publisher and dying of boredom. Maybe I'm crazy—and I'm sure not happy about the War and all—but I'm almost having fun."

Rourke nodded. "I can understand."

"Like two days ago, I needed help. Today—now *I'm* helping. I've done more in the last two days than I ever did in the twenty-eight years I been alive."

"You twenty-eight?"

"Yeah—last month. I look older, right? Everybody tells me that."

Rourke laughed. "I wasn't going to tell you that. You look twenty-eight to me."

"Well," Rubenstein started to say, but Rourke held up his hand and ground the Chevy to a halt. "What is it?"

"Listen," Rourke said. "Gunfire. Just down the road and off to the right there. Sounds like it's from the plane."

He accelerated through the gears, speeding the Chevy down the dirt road they'd been driving along for the last ten miles. Abruptly, he started to slow down, at the same time punching the lights off. As they neared the crash site, he killed the engine. The sound of the gunfire grew louder. He eased the car to the side of the road.

"Paul," he said to Rubenstein. "You want one of my pistols or the rifle?"

"Let me try the rifle."

"Fine." Rourke reached into the back seat, removed the scope cover and showed Rubenstein where the safety lever was. He worked the bolt and introduced a round into the chamber. Fishing in his pockets, he found the two spare five-round magazines for the Steyr-Mannlicher SSG that he had brought along and handed them to Rubenstein. "Just look through the scope. When you see the image clearly—with your glasses on—it should pretty much fill the the scope. Get the crosshairs over your target and squeeze the front trigger. You'll be a terror with it. Come on."

Rourke threw open the driver's door and started for the rocks, Rubenstein behind him. The sound of the gunfire was dying now, and above it, they could hear muted voices calling back and forth to each other. By the time both men had climbed up into the rocks and looked down onto the flatland below, the gunfire had totally ceased.

Rubenstein, beside Rourke, rasped, "Oh my God—we were too late!"

"Yeah," Rourke said, reaching under his coat and stripping a Detonics from under his left shoulder with his right hand. He had two more full magazines with him. "They're starting to move out," he said, peering toward the campsite. As best as he could tell, all the passengers had been killed. The bikers—nearly two dozen of them—were going through the baggage, which they had spread on the ground. He watched as they came to the body of a woman—from the distance, Rourke couldn't be sure, but the blue skirt and the blonde hair made him think it was the stewardess, Sandy Benson. He saw one of the bikers bend over her and take his own glinting Metalifed six-inch Colt Python from the ground beside the woman.

"Give me the rifle," Rourke whispered to Rubenstein.

Taking the SSG, spreading his feet along the ground, and snugging the butt of the stock into his shoulder, Rourke squinted through the telescopic sight, settled the crosshairs on the biker standing by the stewardess, and pulled the first of the twin, double-set triggers. The man stood and whirled around toward the exploding dust behind him. Settling the crosshairs on the biker's forehead, Rourke pulled the rear trigger. He touched the first trigger, the SSG rocked against his shoulder, and the .308's 165-grain boat-tail bullet split the biker's forehead like it was a ripe melon. The man's body fell back in a heap on the ground.

As the other bikers started to react, Rourke speed-cocked the bolt and leveled the Steyr-Mannlicher again. A biker wearing a Nazi helmet was sitting on a three-wheeled bike. Rourke felt he didn't need as much finesse on this shot—he worked the forward trigger all the way through, without using the rear trigger. The helmeted biker threw his hands to his chest and fell back, his bike collapsing to the side as his body hurtled over.

Rourke worked the bolt again. There was a woman biker, her arms laden with belongings of the dead passengers. She was running across the camp. Rourke swung the scope along her path. A bald biker, ruling a big, heavily chromed street machine, was waving frantically for her.

Rourke followed her with the scope as she crossed the camp, past the bodies of the murdered passengers. As she reached out to touch the hand of the bald biker, Rourke fired, killing the bald man with a round in the left temple. He speed-cocked the Steyr's bolt, and swung the scope to the woman. He couldn't hear her above the sounds of the motorcycles revving in the camp area now, but through the scope he could see her mouth opening and closing. He imagined she was screaming. She dropped to her knees, and he shifted the scope downward a few degrees and pulled through on the first trigger. The rifle's gilding metal-jacketed slug skated over the bridge of the woman's nose smashing a crimson red hole into her forehead. Her body snapped back, then her head lolled forward, as though in death she was somehow still praying not to die.

Rourke swapped magazines on the sniper rifle, worked the bolt action, and clipped a biker with bright hair in the right side of his neck. His bike half-climbed a small rise, then rolled over. Rourke worked the bolt again. He swung the scope onto another biker. Like one of his earlier kills, this man was wearing a Nazi helmet. Rourke fired. The Steyr's 165-grain boat-tail soft-point splattered against the right side of the helmet. The biker threw his hands up and fell from his motorcycle. He rolled over and then lay still.

Rourke worked the bolt, swinging the scope along the ground. He spotted another biker in a sleeveless denim jacket with a gang name across its back—the only thing, Rourke thought, that distinguished him. The biker crawled along the ground, then got to his feet and broke into a dead-run for a group of bikers to Rourke's left. Rourke fired and hit the biker in the back. The impact threw the man's body forward on his face into the dirt.

Rourke swung the scope, working the bolt action fast and ripping the last three shots into the group of bikers whom the last man he'd killed had been running toward. Three bodies fell. The other three jumped onto their machines. Rourke swapped magazines on the Steyr and brought the rifle back to his shoulder, firing twice more, killing two more of the bikers as their machines moved out of the campsite.

He brought the rifle down from his shoulder and clicked the safety on.

Rubenstein, lying on the rocks beside him, said, "You just killed twelve men!"

"No," Rourke said. "Eleven men and one woman. Come on, let's see if any of the passengers are still alive down there."

Chapter Thirty Two

Rourke tossed the rifle to Rubenstein and started running along the rocks down toward the campsite. The wind started to whip up from the lower ground, catching the dark Stetson he wore and blowing it from his head. He ran the long fingers of his right hand through his hair, then reached under his coat and snatched out one of the Detonics pistols—in case any of the bikers had survived his fire and decided to return it. As he reached the flat space beneath the rocks, he broke into a crouching run toward the lifeless form of Sandy Benson.

He dropped to his knees beside her, rolled the body of the dead biker away, and leaned over the girl. He raised her head in his hands. She opened her eyes. Her blonde hair fell back from her face, as she looked up and smiled at him.

Rourke said, "Like I told you before—you got a pretty smile, Sandy."

"I knew you'd come—I knew it, Mr. Rourke." Her head fell back, and after a moment, Rourke bent over and kissed her forehead. He closed her eyelids with the tips of his fingers, then rested her head back down on the ground. He found his Python beside her in the dirt, picked it up, and opened the cylinder. All six rounds had been fired. Searching through her purse, he found the two speed loaders he'd left with her and emptied one into the gun, tossing the empty cases into his pocket.

He looked up. Rubenstein had come up behind him. Standing, Rourke blew the sand from the big Colt revolver, closed the cylinder, and stuffed the gun in his waistband.

"I found Quentin—the Canadian. He's dead. I started checking some of the others. I think they're all dead."

"Will you help me here?" Rourke asked, looking down at the dead girl by his feet. "I want to haul all the bodies up by the plane, then torch the plane. We can't possibly bury them."

"The bikers, too?" Rubenstein asked.

"I wouldn't spit on them," Rourke answered.

The grisly task of getting the bodies to the makeshift funeral pyre took more than an hour. Before they set the plane ablaze, Rourke sifted through the passengers' belongings and the things the dead bikers had with them or had left behind. With Rubenstein's help, he placed everything that might be of use to them in a pile in the center of what had been the camp. He told Rubenstein to wait for a few moments, and left. When he returned, he had his flight bag and gun cases. "I stashed these," he said, "back on the other side of the plane."

"You always plan ahead, don't you John?"

"Yeah, Paul," Rourke whispered. "I try to."

Rubenstein was half in shock. He could not get over the mass slaughter committed by the bikers. More than forty people had been murdered for no reason, no sense.

Rourke changed into his own clothes from the flight bag, packing the clothes he'd taken in Albuquerque inside it. He wore a pair of well-worn blue denims, black combat boots, a faded light blue shirt, and a wide leather belt. He squinted toward the rising sun through his dark glasses. About his waist was a camouflage-patterned Ranger leather gunbelt, the Python nestled in a half-flap holster on his right hip. The double Alessi shoulder rig was across his back and shoulders like a vest, magazine pouches for the twin .45's on his trouser belt. The Sting IA boot knife was inside the waistband of his trousers on the left side.

He took his two-inch Lawman Paul had found—the Canadian, Quentin, dead with the little revolver locked in his right fist—and placed it inside his flight bag. He walked over to the bikes left behind by the killers, selected a big Harley, and strapped the flight bag to the back of it. Then he slid his SSG sniper rifle into a padded case and secured it to the side of the bike.

All the time, Rubenstein kept talking. Finally, Rourke turned to the smaller man and said, "Can you ride one of these things, or do you want the car?"

"I'm goin' with you. You're goin' after the rest of the bikers, aren't you?"

"Yeah," Rourke said, pulling the leather jacket on against the pre-dawn cold that still clung to the desert.

"I was thinking about what you said earlier. My parents—in St. Petersburg. Maybe they're alive, maybe they could use my help. And I wasn't much good back there against the bikers. Maybe I could learn to be better. I want to get them, too."

Rourke looked down to the ground. He checked his spare Rolex in the winking sunlight on the horizon. "Let's call it seven-fifteen," he said.

He walked over to the pile of Weapons and accessories by the burnt-out fire. "One of 'ems got my CAR-15," he said absently. He picked up a World War Two-vintage MP-40 submachine gun from the pile, sifted through the debris, and came out with four thirty-round magazines. "Call this a Schmeisser. In the vernacular," he said.

"Can I come with you?" Rubenstein asked.

Rourke smiled and looked over at the younger, smaller man. "Wouldn't have it any other way. Now, like I asked before," and Rourke gestured toward the motorcycles. "You know how to ride one of these things?"

"Nope," Rubenstein grunted, shaking his head.

Rourke sighed hard. "Can you ride a bicycle?"

"Yeah."

"Good. I'll show you how the gears and the brakes work. You'll catch on. Between New Mexico and the East Coast lies more than two thousand miles. You should get the hang of it. Now, give me a hand here."

With Rubenstein helping, Rourke searched the guns that had been dropped by the bikers, scrounging some .38 Special ammo that would work in his .357 revolvers in a pinch and some additional .308 ammo in the process.

"Should I take a handgun?" Rubenstein wondered.

"Yeah—you won't need a rifle. Once I get my CAR-15 back, we'll have two. Here, use this for now." Rourke reached into the pile and found a vintage Browning High Power. "This is a nine-millimeter. One of the best there is. After I get through using this," and Rourke gestured to the German MP-40 submachine gun on the ground beside him, "There should still be plenty of nine-millimeter stuff available."

They siphoned off gas from the other bikes to fill the tanks of the Harley that Rourke had selected for himself and the second Harley he had chosen for Rubenstein. While Rubenstein gathered his belongings and strapped them on the bike, Rourke took the remaining loose ammo from his gun cases—which he was leaving behind—and replenished the magazines for his Detonics pistols and the

Steyr-Mannlicher rifle, packing away the spare magazines for his CAR-15 for when he got it back.

*****

By early morning, Rourke and Rubenstein were ready. Foodstuffs from the airplane were their only provisions. Rourke had checked it all with the Geiger counter. They were low on water, so took the two-day-old coffee as well. Then, filling every container they could find with gasoline from the remaining bikes, they prepared the crashed aircraft for the funeral pyre.

Standing well back, Rourke took a gasoline-soaked rag and started to light it. Rubenstein stopped him.

"Aren't you gonna say anything over them?"

"You do it," Rourke said quietly.

"I'm Jewish, most of them weren't." "Well, pick something, non-denominational," Rourke responded.

Rubenstein, looking uncomfortable, coughed, then began. "The Lord is my shepherd. I shall not want. He maketh me to lie down in green pastures. He leadeth me beside the still waters . . .

Rourke, almost without realizing it, began saying it with him. "He restoreth my soul."

Rubenstein turned and looked at Rourke, and both men went on. "He leadeth me in the paths of righteousness for His Name's sake. Yea, though I walk through the valley of the shadow of death, I will fear no evil, for Thou art with me." Rourke's thoughts were filled with images of Mrs. Richards, and Sandy Benson, whose courage had seemed unending. There was the Canadian businessman whom Rourke had started out disliking—Quentin.

"Thou preparest a table before me in the presence of mine enemies; Thou anointest my head with oil. My cup runneth over."

Rourke thought of the Chicano priest back in Albuquerque and the burn victims there in the church—in his mind he could see the little girl whom he had worked over to save. Then she had died.

"Surely, goodness and mercy shall follow me all the days of my life . . ."

He closed his eyes. Where was Sarah? Where was Michael and Ann at this moment? Were they even alive?

"And I shall dwell in the house of the Lord forever."

Rourke opened his eyes and saw Rubenstein turned to face him. "You've gotten all the rotten jobs, John. It's my turn, now. Give me the torch."

Rourke said nothing, but handed the gasoline-soaked rag to Rubenstein, then the lighter. "Be careful," he said, then watched as the younger man flicked the lighter and touched the flame to the rag. In an instant the rag was a torch and Rubenstein—hesitating for a split second—threw it into the gaping hole in the fuselage.

"Come on," Rourke rasped, his voice suddenly tight and hoarse.

Rubenstein was still standing by the plane, and Rourke walked up to him and put his hand on his shoulder. "Come on, Paul. We got work to do."

Rubenstein looked at Rourke, took off his glasses for a moment, but said nothing. The sound of the flames from the plane was all there was for either of them then to hear.

Chapter Thirty Three

The ride across the desert, trailing the bikers, had been hot. Rubenstein had fallen off the big Harley once but had not been hurt. As Rourke and Rubenstein stopped on a low rise, Rourke turned to the younger man, saying, "I think you're getting the hang of it, Paul. Good thing, too. Look." He pointed down into the shallow, bowl-shaped basin before them.

"My God!" Rubenstein said, shuddering.

In the basin—once a lake bed, Rourke supposed, but now nothing but sand and some barrel cactus dotted here and there—were the bikers they had been trailing. Rourke recognized, even at the distance, two of them from the clothes they wore. One man in particular, whom Rourke had picked as the leader of the gang, wore a Nazi helmet with steer horns jutting from each side, not unlike a Viking helmet. None of the other bikers in the basin had such a helmet. There were at least forty.

"What is it—some kind of convention?"

"What?" Rourke asked absently, then, realizing what Rubenstein had said, he commented, "They were probably part of a larger biker gang and they all set this spot as a rendezvous. Could be more of them coming."

"Damned bikers." Rubenstein spat in the dust.

"Hey—we're bikers, now, aren't we?" Rourke said, looking at Rubenstein. Taking off his sunglasses to clean the dust from them, he went on, "Most bikers are okay—some of them, bad-asses. But you can't generalize. Just 'cause somebody's got a machine under him and he doesn't much care for authority doesn't make him scum. It's just these guys—they're scum."

"But there's gotta be almost three dozen of them down there."

"I make it forty, give or take," Rourke said lazily. He checked his watch, then checked the sun. "In another two hours, it'll be dark. Looks like a good moon tonight, though. We'll get 'em all then."

"There's just two of us," Rubenstein said. "That's twenty-to-one odds."

"Yeah. At least they can't accuse us of taking unfair advantage of them."

"Twenty-to-one, John?"

"Remember what we said over the men and women they killed, back at the plane? 'Yea, though I walk through the valley of the shadow of death, I will fear no evil.' Well, I never cared for fearing things—doesn't help anything much." Then, pointing to the desert behind them, he said slowly, "See all that Paul? Now, that's something we're never going to cross in fear. What's out there in that country after the war, neither of us knows. Nuclear contamination, bands of brigands that'll make these suckers down in the basin look like sissies, probably Russian troops. I don't have the idea that we won the War, really. Good knows what else. There'll be plenty of chances to be afraid later, I figure. No sense starting before we have to."

As quietly as they could, then, Rourke and Rubenstein took their Harleys behind the cover of some large rock outcroppings, ate some of the food they'd brought from the plane, and rested. Rourke told Rubenstein of his plan. When he had finished, Rubenstein said, "You're gonna get killed." Rourke shrugged.

They waited until past sunset and well into the night. The moon was up, and the sounds from the biker camp in the basin indicated to them that everyone was pretty well drunk. While they'd waited, another half a dozen bikers had come into the camp.

Rourke checked both of the stainless Detonics .45's, checking the spring pressure on the magazines, even hand-chambering the first round rather than cycling it from the magazines of the guns. This gave him six rounds plus one in each gun, plus the spare magazines. He secured the Detonics pistols in the double Alessi shoulder rig, then slipped the massive two-inch Colt Lawman inside his trouser belt, at the small of his back. Metalifed like the Lawman snubby, the Colt six-inch Python in the Ranger leather holster on his right hip was checked as well. The Ranger belt had loaded dump pouches, but Rourke was counting on speed if he had to reload. For that reason, he checked the Safarilands cylinder-shaped speed-loaders. There were four of them. Designed for use with the Python, they worked equally as well with the Lawman two-incher. Rourke put two each in the side pockets of his jacket. Taking a swig of the old coffee, he stood up and walked toward his bike.

"I still say you're crazy," Rubenstein warned.

"Could be," Rourke said, settling back, lighting a cigar. "You know, I'm almost out of cigars. Hope we find some place that's got some one of these days." He sucked deeply on the big cigar. "Don't forget to get down there with that Schmeisser when I need you, now."

Rubenstein stuck out his right hand. Rourke looked at him, smiled, and shook it. Then he cranked the bike and headed out from behind the rocks and down into the basin.

The slope into the basin was a long, gentle incline, and he kept the bike slow as he rode it down. Glancing from side to side, his jaw set, the muscles of his neck tensed, he counted perhaps fifty bikers, most of them lying about on the ground. From the brilliance of the moonlight in the clear sky he could see the glint of wine and whiskey bottles strewn about the campsite. He could see the guns—assault rifles of every description, some submachine guns. Virtually everyone was wearing at least one handgun, and several of the bikers were wearing two. As he reached the perimeter of the campsite and started in, he saw some of the bikers get to their feet, watching him. He flashed a smile and waved to one of them. The man waved back, looking at Rourke, but his expression was puzzled.

Rourke kept riding. Not quite halfway to the center of the camp and the man with the Viking helmet, Rourke saw the bikers closing in behind him. He heard a voice in the crowd shouting, "That's Pigman's bike!"

Rourke slowed the bike as he reached the center of the camp. He kept the engine running and stopped less than three yards from the big man with the horned Nazi helmet. He was sitting with his back to his machine. A woman was on each side of him. Rourke took a deep drag on his cigar, smiled, and rasped, "Hello. You the head honcho around here?"

The Viking stood up, hitching his jeans up by the wide black belt slung under his beer pot.

"Yeah. Who are you?"

"We met before, but maybe you don't quite remember," Rourke said, slowly exhaling the gray cigar smoke as he spoke. "My name's Rourke. John Rourke. We were never introduced."

"I ain't met you," the Viking said.

"He's ridin' Pigman's bike!" Someone shouted. Rourke watched the Viking's eyes under the lip of the helmet.

"Like I said. Who are you?"

Rourke, the cigar in the left corner of his mouth, squinted against the smoke and said, "We met back there, where you and your bunch of pussywhips massacred all the people outta that airliner. I'm the guy with the sniper rifle who snuffed out twelve of you assholes. Remember me now?"

The Viking stepped closer toward Rourke. "Yeah. I remember you now. And I'm gonna kill you."

Rourke smiled, whispering, "I just wanted to make sure you knew who I was." His left hand had been resting on the back of the bike seat. Now he flashed it outward, the snubby-barreled Lawman appeared in his fist. He pulled the trigger twice. The muzzle was less than a yard from the Viking's face. Both bullets sliced through his head, and blood and brains exploded, spattering the two women, who began to wail and run.

Rourke gunned the Harley and started into the wall of bikers in front of him, firing the Lawman empty at the nearest of them. He rammed the empty revolver into his belt and got the Python into his right hand, firing.

Rourke cut the Harley forward. The bikers fell away from him like a wedge, the Python roaring into faces and chests and backs. They had been standing so tightly together that missing one was impossible.

As he reached the far end of the camp, Rourke skidded the bike into a tight circle and dismounted. Already, there were bikes revving up from inside the camp. A swarm of the bikers was starting toward him, on foot.

Crouching beside the bike, Rourke speed-loaded the Lawman and the Python and set them comfortably in his hands. Rubenstein should be coming, he thought, opening up with the submachine gun that he'd grabbed from the gear of one of the bikers. He sighted across the Python in his right hand and fired into the attacking bikers. As he emptied the Python and the Lawman into them, gunfire started from above. Rubenstein was shouting above the din—the same counterfeit Rebel yell he'd made back in the garage when they'd got the '57 Chevy started. Rourke used his last loads in the revolvers, firing both guns empty into the bikers, who were running in all directions, dodging the gunfire that rained on them from in front and from behind.

Putting away the empty revolvers as he advanced toward the center of the camp, Rourke snatched up an M-16 from the ground, which had been dropped by a dead biker. Still walking toward the center of the camp, he fired the assault rifle empty, then snatched up a Thompson submachine gun from nearby him on the ground. Walking now, firing three-shot bursts into the masses of bikers around him, he pressed toward the center of the camp. The Thompson clicked empty. He dropped it to the ground, ripping both of the Detonics .45's from their shoulder holsters. He could see Rubenstein now, on his knees beside his bike, at the far end of the camp. The SMG blazed into the bikers around him.

There were half a dozen bikers, mounted, coming toward Rourke now. Most of the others were at the far corner of the camp or already dead. Rourke fired the Detonics in his right fist at the nearest biker, catching the man in the neck and hurtling him from his machine. Then he fired the one in his left fist at a second biker. The bullet hit the biker's face and hammered him to the ground. His bike fell on top of him, the wheels spinning.

Rourke fired both pistols simultaneously as a biker coming up fast from the left started toward him. The biker had a submachine-gun in his right fist, and he was firing. Rourke's twin .45's burned into the biker's chest, ripping the man out of the seat. The biker's ankles locked into the handlebars and the bike spun out into a crowd of bikers ten feet away.

Suddenly, Rourke felt something hammering into his neck. He fell forward, going into a roll, both .45's still in his hands. Three bikers were coming down on him. He fired, each pistol nailing one of the bikers, then coming up empty. As the third biker threw himself onto Rourke, his hands going for Rourke's throat, Rourke palmed the black-chromed Sting IA from the sheath inside his trouser band and drove it down like a stake into the biker's back. Pulling himself up to one knee, Rourke touched his left hand to his neck. His fingers came away covered with blood. Ramming fresh magazines into the Detonics pistols, Rourke got to his feet and continued firing, emptying the guns as he finally reached the center of the camp.

He stopped beside the body of the Viking, and let both pistols drop to his sides. He could see Rubenstein, at the opposite side of the camp, standing, the gun in his hands silent. He squinted, his head aching from the wound on the side of his neck. The basin was a sea of fallen bodies and fallen motorcycles. At the far edge of the camp, he heard the sound of an engine gunning to life and looked up. There was a lone biker, wrestling his machine away from the camp, a trail of dust behind him as he started out of the basin.

Rourke looked down to the ground, snatched up a twelve-gauge riot shotgun which one of the bikers had dropped. Tromboning the pump and chambering a round, Rourke hauled the nearest motorcycle from the ground, straddled it, and started the engine. From behind him, he could hear Rubenstein shouting, "Rourke—what are you doing?"

Rourke headed the motorcycle after the one survivor of the camp and shouted back, "I'm not finished!"

He passed the perimeter of the camp and started picking up speed. The biker's dust trail faded ahead of him. The basin was far longer than it was wide, and at the distant end, toward which Rourke headed, was a steep hill.

Through the dust, Rourke could see his quarry starting up the hill, the bike slipping and the man going down. He jumped up and got the bike under him and tried the hill again. Rourke bent low over the Harley, the wind ripping at his face and hands and hair. His lips were drawn back, his teeth bared, the riot shotgun in his right fist against the controls.

The biker was halfway up the hill, and the bike started collapsing under him again. Rourke skidded to a halt in a cloud of dust at the base of the hill, letting the bike drop to the ground. He snapped the riot shotgun to his right shoulder. He squinted down the sights and muttered the word, "Die!" Then he pulled the trigger.

The biker's hands went to his back, and he fell forward, then slid down the hillside on his face. His body slammed to a halt at the base of the hill, less than ten yards from where Rourke stood.

Rourke dropped the riot shotgun into the sand and started walking back toward the camp. He could see a dust cloud, coming in his direction, a single man on a motorcycle. As the bike neared him, Rourke made out Rubenstein's face and stopped, switching loads in his .45's as he waited.

Rubenstein slowed the bike. Obviously, he was still having a hard time still controlling it. He stopped, and the machine nearly skidded out from under him.

Rourke waited a moment until the dust settled. Then he walked over to Rubenstein and his bike. Rubenstein, very softly, asked, "Are you finished now?"

Rourke nodded his head, saying, "We've got a long ride ahead of us. But I'm finished for now."

VISIT

SPEAKING VOLUMES ON-LINE

National Best-Selling

&

Award Winning Authors

www.speakingvolumes.us